I0619298

The Literary Fantasy Magazine

Volume 1
Issue 1
Winter 2025

Editor-in-Chief: James D. Mills
Fiction Editor: Lee Patton
Submission Reader: Juliette Wallace

Contributing Authors: Alicia Alves, Aubrey Zahn, Courtney Chester, DJ Tryer, Frank William Finney, Grant Sable, James Callan, James D. Mills, John Mueter, Lee Patton, Maria Spence, Menke HB, T.J. Young, and William L. Ramsey.

The Arcanist: Fantasy Publishing

The Arcanist: Fantasy Publishing, LLC

Bloomington, Indiana, United States.

Websites: thearcanist.net | magazine.thearcanist.net

Contact: business@thearcanist.net

Support: support@thearcanist.net

Second Edition, Revised: July 2025

First paperback edition: January 2025

First ebook edition: January 2025

Paperback ISBN: 979-8-9923135-1-2
eBook ISBN: 979-8-9923135-0-5

This page was left intentionally blank
Feel free to write notes here.

Greetings dear readers,

Thank you for purchasing Issue 1 of *The Literary Fantasy Magazine*. We have taken painstaking measures to curate a selection of Fantasy literature that will not only entertain, but provoke thought and evoke emotion. We have tales spanning bloody battlefields, surging seas, ambiguous afterlives, and every landscape in between. Some invite you to laugh, while others might summon darker feelings. There is something for everyone, and always more to learn.

As you read, remember each and every piece in this collection was created by a person, who poured their heart and soul into their craft. Take note of your favorites, and please show them your support! There is a detailed list of contributors at the back of the book, detailing how their other work can be found. In a world full of automated content machines, it is paramount to connect as artists and individuals.

This inaugural issue would simply not be possible without Southern New Hampshire University and the Creative Writing Club therein. Every staff member of *The Arcanist: Fantasy Publishing*, and some contributing authors featured in this issue, are current students or alumni of my beloved university.

Without the help of the kind folks in the CWC, this publication never would have launched. They kindly ran an ad in their newsletter, which found its way to the current staff. So thank you to SNHU, thank you to the CWC, thank you to the contributors for sharing their writing, and thank you—the reader, for giving our stories a home.

Sincerely,

James D. Mills
Editor-in-Chief
The Arcanist: Fantasy Publishing

#07   ENCHANTED

CONTENTS

In order of appearance

After Action Report, William L. Ramsey 1

Fall of Hesperia, T.J. Young 4

Survivor's Guilt, Menke HB 7

Deathmarch in Andante, Grant Sable.. 10

The Bridge, Courtney Chester.. 25

Final Offering, Maria Spence.. 33

Shepherd, Lee Patton 53

Just Before Dusk, Frank William Finney 57

To the Watcher on the Tower, James D. Mills............................... 58

The Value of Horns, James Callan 61

Ahoy There!, John Mueter 68

Sea's Elegy, Aubrey Zahn 81

Journey to the Fetile Land, Alicia Alves ...ı................................ 84

Cretan Quest, DJ Tryer 89

Even the Dead Suffer, Lee Patton 90

Contributors 97

Flash Fiction

Fall of Hesperia, TJ Young.. 4

Survivor's Guilt, Menke HB 7

Shepherd, Lee Patton 53

To the Watcher on the Tower, James D. Mills............................... 58

Sea's Elegy, Aubrey Zahn 81

Short Fiction

Deathmarch in Andante, Grant Sable.. 10

The Bridge, Courtney Chester.. 25

Final Offering, Maria Spence.. 33

The Value of Horns, James Callan 61

Ahoy There!, John Mueter 68

Journey to the Fertile Land, Alicia Alves.................................... 84

Poetry

After Action Report, William L. Ramsey 1

Just Before Dusk, Frank William Finney 57

Cretan Quest, DJ Tryer 89

Serial Fiction

Even the Dead Suffer, Lee Patton 90

Interior Art

Enchanted, Kim Holm vi

Ash, Kim Holm 3

Tranquil, Kim Holm 32

Inktober 2016 (018), Kim Holm 52

Old Troll, Kim Holm 67

Inktober 2016 (026), Kim Holm 80

Inktober 2016 (029), Kim Holm 89

AFTER ACTION REPORT
By William L. Ramsey

Tear stained, scarred, I exited the Orb
      of Rejuvenation at the start of level
      eight, myself again, but there was no
      easy remedy for Queen Boadicea.
      I had been searching for her forever,
      interminably even, when I saw the first

bread crumb in the Temple of Shadows.
      By interminable I do not mean weeks
      or months but most of that afternoon.
      It was right behind the altar in the Sanctum
      of Unmaking. And laying down to sleep
      I soon noticed another. They formed

a line from the curled jade lotus flowers
      to the Athenaeum of Ardor. The sort
      of bread featured in those craft bakeries
      that specialize in firm, thick doughs, breads
      with excessively hard crusts and gaping
      holes through which jams and jellies fall

straight to the saucer, like a sourdough,
      though I could not rule out pumpernickel
      or rye, the light being so dim. It was
      not, let me simply say, the type of bread
      I personally would have chosen to make
      a secret trail with, due to its coarseness

and consistency and the oversized
      crumbs it inevitably produces. Add
      to this the likelihood of pinching off
      larger chunks than usual as a result
      of the anxiety and stress produced
      by being marched under duress by dark

minions of the Shadow Lord to
      the Nexus of Declension, and you get
      a very unsubtle line of bread crumbs.
      Indeed, this effect appeared to grow more
      pronounced as I followed the crumbs deeper
      into the Athenaeum of Ardor. They became

larger and larger until I half expected
>to see a whole bun or loaf awaiting me.
>Discomfiture became complete dismay
>when I found the crumbs were becoming
>increasingly fresh and delicious at each
>step. Crumbs that had been hard and stale

behind the altar, with a hint of charring
>on the crust as if they had been overcooked,
>grew more palatable as I approached
>the gates of the Athenaeum and became
>so pleaant and so perfectly prepared,
>with a hint of cinnamon, that I lost all

composure and rushed forward recklessly
>for the next huge clump, some still warm
>from the oven. This last discovery
>brought me back to my senses. I had feared
>all along that the largeness of the crumbs
>might not escape the attention of her

captors. But if, as I suspected, she had
>begun stopping to make new purchases,
>well, even the most degraded troglodyte
>would surely take notice sooner or later.
>I thus began to fear a trap and, after
>a few more tasty servings, turned back.

fx13   ASH

THE FALL OF HESPERIA
By T. J. Young

The weary knight leaned his battered shield against the ruined wall and sat upon its crumbling parapet. For a long time, he looked out over the rocky plain below. A faint breeze ran cool fingers through his graying, disheveled hair.

Memory, he thought. *Such a painful thing.*

In his mind's eye, an enemy host swarmed the plain, a field overrun with ants. Burning arrows shot through the air. Men screamed. Blood flowed from the parapets. The ground trembled, and thunder rolled in the distance.

But that was not here. No. It was elsewhere.

Bertrand, the legendary Lord of the Marshlands, his lord, had been here with him. Summoned by their ally of old, the King of Hesperia, they rode together in haste to the great kingdom seated in the foothills of the northern mountains. "It will be our last stand," the king had written.

No, the knight thought, *no. I did not come, did I?*

The Lord of the Marshlands was met with fanfare upon his arrival at the castle. Horns blew and flags were flown as Betrand and the knight, and the lord's host, made their way through the gates, clattering into the courtyard, smiling at such a royal welcome. That night, the warriors feasted with the king under warm torchlight, and the princess sang while the minstrels played.

That was not here, but somewhere else. Was it not?

Winter's ice made the parapet treacherous, yet the knight kept watch under heavy skies, moving along the wall, the forsaken sentinel of a dead land. Snow smothered the plain, black trees, gnarled and twisted, bent in futile supplication to the cruel winds. There was a cave, he recalled, high up in the mountains where the king's treasure was hidden, glittering chests of gold. Gold that he coveted.

Just a rumor. A myth. It was not me.

The winds shifted. The knight stopped, faced away from the wall and gazed into the ravaged courtyard. They lost so many in the battle; Josiah the Bald, Edgar and his twin sons, Lord Morgan... Proud, they stood in his memory as idols—

No. Sacrifices. All of them gone.

The old knight hung his head. Cold winds tore at his face as he ran his hand over the crumbling stones. In his mind, he could see Morgan in the courtyard, armor caked with gore, helmet gone, his sword flailing like some mad thing. He was surrounded, overwhelmed, lost beneath the enemy's onslaught.

Wait. Did not Morgan survive? Surely, I saw him, years later, crossing the Torandor.

Another memory came to him. A day of sunshine, of warmth, lying in the grass. And the king's daughter—Princess Aurora. Her face gleamed like the inside of a seashell. The forlorn knight felt the sun on his face, smelled the sweet scent of daisies, and saw clouds sail in the breeze, phantom ships on a sea of eternity.

No, no, no. He shook his head. *That was much later, somewhere else.*

A tired sigh escaped the knight as he pinched the bridge of his nose. Returning to his shield, he took it and left the wall, descending the broken stairway into what remained of the courtyard. Where there were once carts and horses, men in resplendent armor, there were now only cracked flagstones, dirt, and the howl of the wind.

The roof of the main hall had collapsed. The knight picked his way over the stones to where a remnant of the floor still lay intact. Part of a mosaic could be seen there. He swept away the grime and debris obscuring the image—a blue horse, rearing, against a backdrop of tall trees, a garland of acanthus leaves surrounding it. *The seal of Hesperia.*

A vision came to him. He was in a darkened hall at night. Spears and axes hung on the walls. A man in a leather cape was speaking, his face dark and hard as iron. "We'll be there," he said, "when the signal comes, and the gates open, we'll come through. Then the gold will be yours…"

A bolt of pain shot through the knight.

No, that was not me… Not me.

An echo drew his attention to the far end of the hall. A portion of the gallery was still protruding from high on the wall. A man stood there, looking down at him. The knight stepped closer, strained his eyes to make out who it was. The man wore a doublet of fine cloth, woven in a pattern of waves. *It cannot be.*

Lord Bertrand.

The old knight knelt and bowed his head. But his voice caught in his throat, and before he could speak, a fire suddenly broke out, roaring upwards. Flames licked at the gallery. It collapsed, Bertrand falling with it, crashing onto the stones below.

No. The knight furrowed his brow. *That did not happen. Did it?*

He scrambled over to where the lord had fallen, then found himself reeling backwards through time, back to that horrifying day, that hell, when the enemy horde stormed through the open gates, slaughtering all in their path. He saw the king's head mounted on a pike, the princess' body splayed open, a doll torn apart. *Aurora!*

"No, no!" the knight cried through choked sobs. "That was not here. It was not me. I did not open the gates!"

Bertrand's face was caked with blood, one eye missing, his legs twisted, shattered. But his remaining eye opened, looked at the knight. The lord's lips moved, and the broken knight bent closer to hear his words.

"I forgive you," Bertrand whispered.

Oh god! the knight thought, tears streaming down his face. *That is not what he said to me. No!* His fists slammed onto the ground. *There was nothing to forgive …*

The weary knight stood, his face a mask, picked up his shield and slowly made his way through the castle ruins to the gate. He looked out over the plain.

It was not me. I was never here.

Survivor's Guilt

By Menke HB

His boots sank deep into the sludge. The after-effects of a ravaging were always grim, but this one had been singular in the horror left behind. The smell of burned and decaying flesh repulsed him, yet buried memories tugged on his muscles like a magnet. Rao'wan took a blood-stained handkerchief from his satchel and wrapped it tightly around his scaly nose. Then he limped into the village. His village.

The silence was stifling. He wanted to hum, but the supralabial scales around his mouth refused to grant him a melody. Coming to the charred remains of the Mother's fountain, he closed his eyes and wept. For a moment, he could again hear the bells of the temple calling the women to prayer; the men rowdily returning from their day in the fields; the children playing no-fly-tag in the square. At sixteen, he had left it all behind.

That fateful day, both he and Nas'hir, his senior by four minutes, had been called upon by the High Priestess. From all the males in their hatch cycle, they had been chosen to serve the Mother by tending the temple's graveyard, the sacred grove where all who lived in service of the Great Dragon were laid to rest. Nas'hir had accepted the task wholeheartedly. Rao'wan had echoed his assent without conviction. He wanted a wife, a family. Not a life of silent service to Bachmathu— may her wings ever grow stronger—no matter how much honor the position would grant him. Six hours later, he had packed his satchel and abandoned his people.

Rao'wan trudged on, forcing his injured leg to carry its burden. Entering the temple courtyard, he bowed his head. Only the north and east walls were left standing, yet even without doors barring his entry, he refused to defile the sanctuary. He had not fallen so far as to break the most sacred rule: only women were allowed in the Temple proper. Instead, he took the path through what had once been the gardens.

Without the obvious presence of death, there was still some peace left in the uprooted plants, the blackened trees. When he spotted a single thistle blossom amidst the ashes, Rao'wan removed his handkerchief. The flower did little to dissuade the smell of utter destruction, but he clung to this tiny signal of hope before continuing through the crumbled archway, past shattered statues and upended graves, until he came to the meadow. The chapel still stood. His fingers caressed its rough, uneven stones. He could have lived here. *This* could have been his home. *Would it really have been worse than his decades of wandering?*

He tried the handle. The wood fit so snug within the surrounding stone, he had to thrust with his shoulder to force it open. Instantly, he regretted taking off his handkerchief. He reached for it, then faltered. Whatever reality awaited him here, he ought to face it snout open. Rao'wan ought to face the destiny he had unwittingly escaped.

It did not take Rao'wan long to find the source of his discomfort. A corpse, flesh lacerated and scattered, sat slumped before the altar. *Had he even defended himself?* His clothes lay in tatters around him. He pulled a large black feather from a damp strip of leather. Harpies. Of course they had come. They would have been the first to pick through the scraps once the fires died down.

For a moment, Rao'wan hesitated. The Mother had not gifted him with a high capacity for magic. One chance would be all he got. Looking around the room, he found a torch and lit it. He nearly retched as he lifted the corpse and peered into its empty sockets. "Mother, forgive me," he mumbled. Then he severed the skull from Nas'hir's ravaged body.

Taking a thin piece of jade, a dagger, two sticks of incense, a flat rock, and an apple out of his bag, Rao'wan set to work. He put the skull atop the rock in the center of the altar. Then he took the apple and stuck the incense in it, carefully, so it formed a perfect "V" before setting it behind the skull. Last, prying open the jaw, he placed the jade on what was left of his friend's tongue.

Closing his eyes, he felt for the well of magic inside him. He had seldom called upon it these past twenty-eight years. But now, now he had need of it. *Now he had need of her.* Once he felt the magic burning in his throat, he took the dagger, slashed the inside of his wing and spoke in a deep, earthy roar, "Mother, hear my call." Then he breathed out, lighting the incense and scorching the skull's remaining flesh.

As he opened his eyes, his shoulders released some of the tension they had borne since Rao'wan resolved to return. It worked! Within Nas'hir's smoldering remains, the gem was glowing and emerald specks of night fire danced where his gray eyes once sat.

"Why have you come? Rao'wan, son of—"

The skull's hoarse question was interrupted by a strangled gasp.

Rao'wan watched the glow dim. *No.* He shut his eyes once more, grasping for the threads of his dissipating spell. No matter how much he yearned to stitch them back together, he could not do it. He had come all this way to beseech Nas'hir, to gain closure. Now his brother's maw would remain silent forever.

As the last glow vanished, he swore under his breath and pulled out his dagger once more. Friend or foe, he would silence the one who had caused the distraction.

"Come out and face me like a Dragon." Rao'wan's voice echoed through the chamber.

As the small silhouette stepped into the torchlight, trembling, he dropped the knife. Before him stood a hatchling. She could not be older than five or six, yet here she was, a survivor of his people. *By the Great Dragon*. He fell to his knees, swore a solemn vow.

"Mother, I will not fail you again."

DEATH MARCH IN ANDANTE
by Grant Sable

It was three in the morning. Len was awake, but exhausted, just as she was every witching hour since her twin sister's death. She was curled in bed, staring at an old photograph of the two of them playing their instruments on the beach. Voices dripped into her ear like snakes in a well. She spun around, searching the room lit only by a faint indigo glow. There was no one.

The words were faint and overlapping at first, ramping to a deafening drone until suddenly clicking together clearly: *At the heart of the cathedral, find the doors to the afterlife.*

Len clutched the photograph to her chest. "Eloise?"

The voice went quiet. Even so, she knew it was her. Who else would whisper their wish through the graves, if not El? The thread connecting the twins reached from the underworld and tugged at her ankles. Len decided to become that thread's willing marionette, holding scissors below a knot she tied.

Len adorned her neck with a loaded pendant pistol and rose to stand tiptoe on her bed, gripping the frame of the skylight. Every door in her waterside cottage creaked with the degeneration of a century, but that skylight always kept her secrets. It swung open without a sound, and Len pulled herself through the portal into heavy, midnight air. For a creature of the night like herself, this was almost an outing like any other.

A casual stroll to the afterlife isn't much different from the usual.

Len leapt from the molding roof of her family's shack on top of her neighbor's bungalow, the moonlit street blurring beneath her. Wraithlike, she carved a path from one roof to another, manifesting a bridge only she could traverse. She seemed to glide through the air between landings, the indigo nightgown she'd been wearing all day billowing in her wake. Warm wind whirled the long waves of her lavender hair, carrying the shrieks of swallow-tailed gulls—the only other living souls about the island town of Belgram at this hour.

She crested over hills of damp grass and fields of white orchids, petals the color of burial gowns raining on her arms covered in gooseflesh. Cottages kindled yellow lights into the blue, spiraling heavenward. The black mourning candles lining their windows congested her lungs with smoke. Climbing closer and closer, her heartbeat rose with the elevation, and her creeping fatigue quickly evaporated. It was foolish raising her hopes prematurely, but what else could explain the ghostly presence she felt drawing near?

As Len approached the cathedral, she looked back for the first time since leaving her house. An unmatched view stretched before her. The dawn goddess's house of worship had been built on a steeply arching cliff closest to the sky. She fancied the whole structure would soon crumble into the ocean, taking the island's religion with it. From here, Len could spy the entirety of Belgram. The café, where El had composed poetry over sunflower tea. Their high school, where El's violin had enchanted the concert hall. The festival grounds, where El's body had been found in the arms of the dusk god.

* * *

After her twin's death, Len sealed herself from the world. She spent the first day in bed, smothering herself with a pillow to drown out the doorbell. It was dark when she realized she hadn't eaten since the night before. She sneaked out the skylight, as she did most nights, and patronized the midnight market to replenish groceries. When she got back, Len posted a note on the front door telling casserole bearers to bring their gifts to a homeless shelter, then she phased out of existence, as though jumping into a private dimension.

Len spirited away, going wherever the wilds would welcome her. She spent most of her time in the forests at the edge of town, sitting cross-legged behind the island's waterfalls. Sometimes she climbed a hill to render the vistas in her sketchbook, penciling in sunflowers where there weren't any, planting their seeds in those spots once she'd finished.

Len only bade farewell to the palms and returned home when the town's eyes weren't open to watch her, then set back out before they were. She did this for nearly a week. Had she family for support, she might've had the strength to weather the mourners and police, both leaving messages about their sympathies and theories. But Bishop Hayes, her holy father, left her to the vultures; casting away, strung out on the family boat until the sun went down. He hadn't drunk since joining the church, but he was emptying his pill bottles faster than normal. Len dipped into them too. He might've noticed.

One morning in the den, Len rummaged through a desk for her sketchbook. She was surprised to find not only hers, but another. She held a discolored green tome with a still life fruit basket and "Eloise Hayes" in cursive on the front. Strawberry perfume lingered on the paper. Len delicately unearthed it, taking it to her room where she flopped on her bed, holding it to the sky. Quick sketches of office supplies on the first page, detailed renders of household plants on the second, and a surprisingly flattering portrait of Len on the third, aside from the overdrawn ears, which were far bigger than they should be. After that, blank.

The raw talent was there, unrefined. Her sister had always groaned wistfully about wanting to draw more, but besides the music they played together, El considered hobbies, and the idea of a well-rounded existence, to be indulgences. El's modus operandi had been sacrificing today's happiness for the future's: spending weekends deciphering waterlogged textbooks in the crumbling library, declining ferry tickets to the mainland in order to cram for exams, signing up for the more practical Spanish when what she wanted to learn was Latin.

Len told herself she wouldn't live that way, servile to the future. She couldn't be chained down by the past either, but what did that leave her? An impulse flashed through her nerves, and she snatched her messenger bag, sweeping through the cottage, bewitched. Len foraged through cabinets, drawers, below the kitchen sink, looting every nonperishable and survival implement she spotted. When her frenzy dwindled to shallow breaths, and the pantry stood empty, she dropped the bag on her bed. Clothing. Flare gun. First aid. Fresh water. Canned meats, fruits and vegetables. Garden sandwiches her friend, Hye-Mi, brought last night. A pillow with her Victorian doll, Grace, packed inside.

The only thing left was the family boat. Len would set sail, live a life big enough for both her and El; play piano concertos for swooning audiences, summit the coastal mountains, and melt into their flower fields at twilight, weaving dream catchers until the nightmares stopped strangling her from sleep.

It wasn't reckless, but respectful, an honor to the memory of rebellion. Ever since they were children, El's saintly disposition had always tempted Len to shock her with little acts of sin. Caper necklaces from the jeweler, bathe nude in the café's pond, make blood sacrifices to the dusk god, and now, captain a pirate a ship, leaving their birthplace behind.

One last time. She would visit her classmates one last time, a silent toast to their years together, then she was gone.

* * *

Returning to her high school felt like she was walking through a dark mirror of reality. The building looked as it always had; finely carved dark wooden walls, off-white marble floors accented with streaking black flecks, the dim chandeliers populated with flickering bulbs. What it housed, however, was unrecognizable. Students traveling in packs and conversing in whispers, conspicuously segregated by which city district they were from. Teachers standing outside classrooms holding clipboards, eyes darting to track the students like prison guards. Even the garden, once a haven for the student body, felt the touch of corruption: beyond its frosted glass, blackened limbs tangled like vines in sentient support networks, and the soil lay bare. The atmosphere was that of a storm shelter. If she didn't know better, she would think another flood was in the forecast.

Heads turned, one by one, latching onto Len. Feet started, then stopped, throats cleared then closed. She touched her neck, made sure she wasn't bleeding. That might be why everyone was staring, but probably not. Even, if she hadn't disappeared for the last week, the students there were strangers to crime. Death only came to Belgram one at a time from natural causes or swept in droves from tidal waves and earthquakes.

The worst crime committed in the last five years was last summer when Len broke into the school to release a swarm of crabs. Murder just wasn't in anyone's lexicon. It didn't help the killing was premeditated, ornamental. It wasn't some home invasion or back-alley mugging gone awry; it was a spectacle, a statement. Of what, no one knew. The waterwheel of rumors likely spun freely, but Len shut herself from speculation. No explanation would ease her mind, so there was no point looking for one.

As Len rounded the cylindrical chamber of the garden, most of her peers gave her a wide berth. There were a few condolences and touches on the shoulder, but an otherwise clear path to the north wing.

Locker 181's mahogany vents overflowed with letters and the flowers plucked from the garden. Petals wilted and dropped, some floating down the narrow, shallow waterway that ran along the hallways' edges, and others smoldering in the cluster of black candles. Her fingers ghosted over 181's lock. The twins knew each other's combinations by heart; they used to leave each other treats, like test answers or butterflies. Sometimes tricks, like wrong test answers or jumping spiders. Len resisted the temptation to read the letters, instead spinning the dial of her own locker and loading the books within into the pillowcase she carried slung over her shoulder.

This was everyone's way of saying goodbye ... that's between them and El. Len's time to say goodbye would come, she knew. One day.

She thought she'd navigated these turbulent waters already, when Mom died. But what she'd been learning with the burial of every pet, the final voyages of every old friend to the mainland, was that there was no universal process for grieving. Every life is unique, and so their sudden absence leaves behind a new cave, and a new way to escape the void.

An icepack helps ease a sprained calf muscle but won't do anything to help a broken shin. Losing others didn't mean that she had any idea how to lose El. Though one thing had been universal: when she lost others, El had always been there.

Come first period, she sat beside a vacant desk. It was the most sought after in the classroom; the sun hit it perfectly without blinding you, and it was right next to the bird fountain, so finches would hop onto your notebook and steal your pens. El won it in a poker tournament on the first day of school, and their classmates always circled it like piranhas. Now, they scattered as koi after a rock plunged into their pond.

The lecture on the phases of mitosis was complete gibberish to Len, and without her sister there to answer questions, she was forced to christen her biology textbook. The pages stuck together, and pungent mildew sprouted at their edges. The moment the bell rang, she walked straight to the next period alongside a body of phantom limbs.

Being at home without El, Len had grown accustomed to—or at least, she understood the theory behind it. One bowl for breakfast and eat it on the dock. Talk to an empty bed, don't wait for a response. Shower until the steam is suffocating, then crank up the heat. Nothing felt right, but she was practiced. School was a new script to learn, a new circle of hell to build a nest in, as was every once-shared stomping ground on the island. She thought of the boat, the unfamiliar scenes ahead that bared no memories.

For over three years, Len took her lunches in the seminary room, but today it was locked up. It was her father's classroom, and he wasn't speaking with the goddess anymore—not after she had relinquished two of his girls to the dusk. Instead, Len traded her nightgown for a one-piece swimsuit and broke into the pool with a stolen key. Father and El prattling on about the Twilight Text during lunch had always made her feel left out anyway. She curled her feet around a ladder rung and swayed in the water, sipping cold black coffee from an earthenware mug and feasting on the last sunfish the twins had caught. Rain pelted the swim building's glass dome, and clouds obscured the gray sky like shadow puppets, creating a canopy of pale sunlight and negative space bobbing on the water.

A metal shriek suddenly raced through the lanes. Piercing cold blew in. A gangly form darkened the doorframe of the front entrance, now thrown wide.

Len tensed and reached for her pistol, only to remember it was at home.

"Whoever did this is still out there," her father had said when entrusting it to her, "and they might come back to—"

Finish the job.

But the intruder stepped into sight, and it was only Young Song, the mayor's eldest. Lady-killer, but not a regular killer.

"G'morning, Len."

He didn't wait for a response before sitting cross-legged at the opposite end of the pool. He stretched one of his toned arms into the water, dipping it back out, staring at a drop catching the sun on his index finger. A faint sweat dampened his black hair, and his one-size-too-big Belgram Sailors jersey hung from his light-golden skin.

Her mistake for not locking up. Now that he was here though, she didn't have the energy to ward him away. She refused to look him in the eyes, instead glowering into her coffee, but its color reminded her of them anyway. Not like there was any point bothering—nothing could scrape the feeling of eyes from her skin. Even when she tried to sleep, there were faces staring at her; in her closet, hanging between the gowns, in the corner, poking from behind the mirror, on the ceiling, blinking through the skylight.

"I put a bell on my sister's door," Young said, flicking a droplet from his finger, ringing an imaginary bell, "and I sleep with a bat under my pillow. Don't even know why we own one. Not like this island has a baseball diamond." His voice was slow and thick, lacking its characteristic sharpness. He had dark bags under his eyes, as if he hadn't slept for days.

Len forked a bite of fish into her mouth, hoping that if he saw her eating, he'd think she was managing and leave her be. It was undercooked. "And Hye-mi's okay with that?"

"The bell?" he rolled his neck, cracking the air. "Not really. She says it makes her feel like a cat. But what else am I supposed to do?"

Nothing. If this happened to someone else, Len would have put one on her and El's door. Hang one from El's collar, even, above the amber locket. Her sister wouldn't like it any more than Young's did, but the next thing Len knew, she'd probably wake up with a chime of her own.

"Never seen you swim," Young said.

"Trying something new," she leaned back to drink the last of her bitter brew.

"You won't do it. You're too sentimental."

Len's throat paralyzed, coffee trickling down. Her dark-purple lipstick imprinted the earthenware rim. Only when the liquid burned did she finish swallowing. "Won't do what?"

"Leave the island."

She tipped the empty mug back to hide her expression, faking a gulp. "Who said I wanted to?"

"People here get in the water for one reason," he stretched his swim jersey emphatically. "To get off this island."

The pressure of three meters of water was probably preferable to the pressure of being next in line for mayor, now that he mentioned it. But there was a reason for him to resurface now.

"Whose daddy will you tell? Yours, or mine?" Len closed her eyes and sank into the pool, rinsing her neck with the encroaching water.

Young crinkled his brow and leaned forward. "I know you think there's nothing left in Belgram, but—"

She ignored him, continued her descent. Her ears were halfway submerged when Young shouted, his voice gargling through the water. "Your sister won't be the last one! We both know whoever did this won't stop with her."

The hair floating around Len like a jellyfish suctioned to her skin as she shot up. Chlorine burned her nostrils and water rushed her lungs. She rearmed her glower and choked out: "Is that supposed to be reassuring?"

One of the crabs she'd turned loose scuttled around the pool, testing the water with a claw.

Young put his mouth to his knuckles and spoke softly. "You won't be alone in this for long, I mean."

I'm not alone, but she buried the thought. In his state, her father held no presence in her life. If he noticed the locked seminary, Young probably knew that. That didn't mean company would help anything. The only one who could bring reprieve was El.

That was how it had always been between them: Len was the knight, shielding El from danger, and El was the nurse, softening Len's scars. Len would build her a blanket fort when a storm was coming, watch movies before her to find out if the dog died, pull a knife on anyone who gave her a hard time. And El would brew her hot chocolate when the fort collapsed, bring her tissues when the dog *did* die, bandage her when the other person also had a knife. Len didn't need someone else take on her pain, she wanted the chance to take on El's.

It should have been me.

Everyone knew Len was the rotten one, but that wasn't the kind of sentiment you voiced unless you wanted to be carted to the psych ward. So, she clamped her mouth and kept that pearl inside.

Young dropped his legs into the pool, still wearing his shoes and socks, and patted the space between. His mouth curled into a warm, shy smile. "C'mere."

She averted her gaze, crossing her arms.

"I won't bite. I'm a Sailor, not a shark, remember?"

Len sighed and furled into a half-moon, kicked off the wall, and butterfly stroked down the lane.

She nestled her head in his lap, sweeping wet tentacles from her brow. She held back a contented sigh and pushed her hand into his palm. It reminded Len of how El used to sit, singing on the pier, legs dangling in the surf, brushing her doll's hair until the sun drowned. Except Young wasn't singing a lullaby, and Len couldn't if she wanted, her throat wet and hoarse. The best she could do was murmur: "The police say it was a one-time thing. A disgruntled citizen making a statement about the merger."

He stroked her hair in silence for a long moment, let her sit with the feeble pretense.

"If you were me . . ." he began, bending down to whisper in her ear, ". . . would you take down the bell?"

* * *

They found her nine nights ago, at the grand opening festival for Nascent Junction.

Belgram had flourished through diamond mining until a few years back, when a tidal wave flooded out most of the mines, bringing the industry to its knees. That forced the upper and lower-class districts to cooperate. Even though the divide was supposedly washed away by the waves, the districts wanted to solidify their newfound alliance. So, for the past year, an impromptu committee of bleeding hearts toiled away to restore the site hit the hardest, a quaint business sector near the shoreline. Finally, it was ready: Nascent Junction, suture to the town's rift.

The main attraction of the eve was the unveiling of twin dawn and dusk god statues, matron and patron deities of the upper and lower districts, presiders over this world and the next. Naturally, Len was a follower of the dusk god. El, on the other hand, worshipped the dawn goddess, even though their family was from the lower district. Either way, both were looking forward to the unveiling. The whole town was—every islander not shackled by old age or resentment for the union planned to make the fest that night.

With limited resources, they couldn't bring the Junction into the twenty-first century. It bordered the sea like a gothic castle town fit to vanish beneath the tide and color the pages of storybooks. Even so, that didn't stop people from enjoying the festivities. Red and blue banners strung between stone parapets like rows of teeth, and vendor wagons carted the storefronts. Children—and high schoolers with the hearts of children—bounded through the streets with sparklers, fizzling flames in the temperate blackness and dropping the smell of spent fireworks. If El had been there, Len would've bought her a sparkler.

El promised to meet Len at 9 PM on the dot. She said she wanted to pray for the districts' unity at the cathedral first. Nine-thirty came and went. El only had a single tardy in her high school career, and it was from stopping to rescue a turtle with a cracked shell.

"Probably just ran into some friends and lost track of time," their father mused, adjusting the cuffs on his robes. *He was thinking of the wrong twin.* Len tried pointing that out, but he simply sent her away with a crisp bill and a recommendation to "try the shooting gallery, it's really something," leaving her to be the parent, like always. Many tighten the reins on their loved ones after one of them slips away; he let the reins slack. Losing his wife had cracked his faith, but it had been rebuilt strong, and now he thought nothing could happen to his daughters—like lightning, true misfortune didn't strike twice.

That was the last night he believed bad luck had a limit.

Len anxiously scanned her phone every time she started to relax, but her calls to El went to voicemail and nothing came back, although that wasn't much of a surprise. El left her phone at home most days. Technology frightened her; she preferred the familiarity and stability of nature. Flowers didn't jump scare her if she clicked the wrong petal, leaving her huddling for safety in Len's bed.

Len wandered the fair in search of El like an earthbound spirit, tugging their classmates' sleeves to ask if anyone had seen her. At one point she was about to hike to the cathedral, but a young churchgoer skipping from that direction insisted it was empty. With a minute until ten, the moment everyone was waiting for, Len slumped on the edge of the fountain in the junction square—a replica of the great tree that once marked the boundary between the districts, water spouting from its branches. The tips of Len's hair brushed against its roots. Her feet were weak and blistered, and a fragrant noodle stand tormented her empty stomach.

Where are you, El?

A rousing voice boomed over a microphone and the crowd filtered out of the square, congregating in the amphitheater up north like paper lanterns set adrift.

One of the lanterns bent down in front of her, drooping her black bob into the collar of her lace button-up. Hye-mi Song. Only chains of rubies on her throat—sparkling, not chiming. Her friend group, knit just tight enough to bundle Len up on occasion, halted their course once it dawned Hye-mi wasn't aboard. She put her hands on her knees and blinked wide eyes, lamblike in her regard and rhythm of speaking. "Aren't you coming, Len?"

Len shook her head, twisting her sapphire locket, scouring it for sight of her sister as if it were a crystal ball.

Hye-mi frowned. "Did something happen? Where's El?"

"Haven't seen her," Len's stare wandered from the gemstone to the stars, making no stops to register the girl.

"Do you need help finding her?" she asked, leaning in and examining Len like a patient. Hye-mi's own affairs were never in order, but she always made time to look after those of others. Probably why Young fretted like he did.

One sibling always ends up the other's keeper, don't they?

Only then did Len wake to the reality of what a downer she was being. She forced a smile, failing to stretch it to her eyes. "We'll be fine. Go enjoy the festival with the others, okay?"

Hye-mi glanced at her crew, then back at Len, biting her lip and bouncing on her heels. The townspeople's rowdy cheers erupted in the distance. "You'll really be alright?"

"Don't worry. She probably just ran into some friends and lost track of time." Len waved Hye-mi off and she jogged after her friends, glancing over her shoulder on the way.

Feigning just that moment of mirth drained Len, and she doubled over into her lap, resisting the urge to tip back and let the fountain swallow her.

Not a minute later, the screams started.

Len jumped to her feet and ran toward them. The once-empty square was now flooding with patrons fleeing the amphitheater. When the statues were almost in sight, Hye-mi stepped out and blocked her path.

"Len, don't!"

Hye-mi was strong, but Len pushed as hard as she could and broke through her bastion.

Every twisted nightmare she'd been dreading was conjured to life. The statue of the dusk god, cradling her younger twin. White sundress draping over black marble, yellow hair sagging over colorless skin. Her beloved sister, with a slit throat and a blood-stained amber locket.

* * *

"Remind me why you insist on the organ?" El asked.

"Because …" Len said, holding the lowest note, echoing it off the cathedral walls "It's like the piano, but goth."

"Of course. Why didn't I think of that?"

El's face was bent over her violin, but Len could tell she was smiling. The cathedral radiated bright orange in the summer sunset, haloing her in a burning light.

"'Heavenly Again' really does sound nicer with a piano though, you know?" El continued. "We could use the one in the concert hall."

"I know that. But who else would perform it like this but us?" Len threw her hair back and kicked a heel up in the air, shadows skittering dramatically while she played a flourish.

"So, it's about showing the world something they've never seen?"

"Something like that. Isn't there anything you want to show people with our music?"

"There is, actually." El sat on the organ bench next to Len, swinging her legs back and forth. "Mom."

Len blinked in surprise. "Mom?"

El smiled and nodded.

* * *

Hye-mi eventually overpowered Len, pulling her away from the sight. Len stopped struggling, went slack in her arms. She didn't know where their father was. At that point, she didn't care. It didn't matter whether it was his failure, hers, or the goddess's. El had slipped through all of their fingers on her way down.

The officer on the scene rifled through papers and read her questions from scripts, questions she didn't remember with answers she wasn't cognizant of. When they drove her home to search the cottage, Len waded into the surf out back, bathing in police lights spinning like red-and-blue lighthouse beams. Len didn't believe in twin-telepathy— Len picked up on El's secrets, El had always been a bad liar, and sometimes Len feigned a prophetic vision to spook her. But she didn't believe. Regardless of how much she scrubbed at her neck, Len couldn't shake the feeling she was bleeding.

* * *

Nine nights after El was murdered, the night Len stood facing the front of Belgram Cathedral in her night gown, her throat finally felt clean. The family boat was safely docked, messenger bag beneath the boards. Her voyage awaited. Young was wrong. But the voice was right. There was something inside.

For Len's rejection of the dusk god, the shrine yawning open had never been a welcome sight. Tonight, however, the tower's clockface was not the divines' eyes watching her in judgment; its bell chimed twelve to mark the hour, not to count her sins.

The front doors swept the gray stone of the interior, grinding shut behind her. Round windows beside each pew smuggled pockets of light to invite escape from the overwhelming holiness, while black candles waxed their ledges, coiling smoke through the humid air. The marble relief of the goddess slept high in the back, flowing hair of her bust fixed to a stained-glass window. There was no sound within the sanctuary—not of the waves, the gulls, nor her own breathing. But there was a presence, the only true divine presence Len had ever known. El.

Len shouted El's name, and every echo was a hollow reminder of her absence. Her eyes desperately scoured the pews row by row for sunrise hair, skipped across the windows for sight of a smiling face. Her focus on minute details was so tight, she almost didn't pick up on the shark in the water: a pair of double doors towering at the far end, picturesque twins of stained glass where their father had once preached. Their presence was so organic she briefly wondered if they had always been there.

She rose onto her toes, breath swelled in her chest, and a grin broke ground on her face. Her sister wouldn't lie. This was her promise. Maybe there was another world on the other side, far from this one, where no one could touch them. She dashed down the aisle's red rug how children raced across the beach to a flag in the sand. Gripping both handles at once, she wrenched them open and burst through the threshold.

There was no new world. Only the same organ, the same window, the same relief. The spell was broken. The hypnotist's fingers snapped, and the crippling weight of reality surged back to smother her. She wrapped her arms about herself and let her spine slack, head hanging and elbows tucking in, nursing the chasm in her stomach.

"Len!"

She whirled toward the voice, and at the entrance was a figure haloed in black. There was no explanation for it but a fragile dream at the fringes of sleep, the slightest disturbance away from waking. Her heart stopped, and she willed it not to beat again, not to signal the passing of this moment.

But her chest was already pulsing, and the doors were closing. By the time she could reach them, could even glimpse her up close, the locks had clicked.

"Eloise!" Len shook the handles rapidly, knowing they wouldn't budge. With the doors blockading the alcove and the window's latch out of reach, she was in a prison of stained glass.

The figure caught up, and though only warped colors and silhouettes shined through the prismatic panes, there was no mistake: sunflowers tucked behind each ear, the Twilight Text strapped to her belt, and her favorite sundress flowing to her knees. The amber was clean.

Shadowed hands jostled the door in vain, then reached toward her, touching the glass. "You came for me …"

Len mirrored her palms on the other side, and swore she felt her warmth. "Of course. I would never leave you."

El started sniffling, and Len blinked her own tears away, shaking her head and forcing a brave face. They could only afford one of them falling apart right now, and dying had staked El the greatest claim. It was left to Len to reunite them, and there was no chance she wouldn't take.

She reached into her nightgown and ripped the pendant pistol out, clenching the trigger and aiming at the door. "Stand back."

"Wait!"

Len lowered the gun and spoke in a slow, hopeful voice. "It's okay. I'm going to break out of here, and then we can be together."

El's fingers curled like claws. "Before you do anything … can we play a song?"

"El, I—"

"Just one song, please?" El's voice broke.

Len sighed and tucked the pistol back in, clinking it against the sapphire. Nine rotations of the Earth without her sun. Five more minutes barely compared to that eternity. "'Heavenly Again?'"

El dried her cheeks and nodded. A smile crinkled Len's eyes. "No" wasn't a card in Len's deck when it came to El, but her reactions always made it worthwhile.

Once, when they were little, while the sun was out for El's half of the birthday, her wish was for their family to reenact her favorite fable, "The Goat Princesses." Of course, she quickly decided an outdoor performance would be better since more people could enjoy it, and half the lower district ended up caught in her scheme. There was great resistance, mainly because El had terrible taste in literature, and it was intensely shameful for the performers. But the children begrudgingly got into character once they were subjected to El's trademark wounded-lemur eyes. Parents scrambled to fashion makeshift costumes and sets, and everyone came away with fond memories. Best of all, though, was how El's face lit up at every turn, how she hung off her chair, gasped earnestly at twists she'd read a hundred times, and thanked everyone with crushing hugs from her tiny arms.

Mom shipwrecked a few months later, and at the funeral, Len swore to never let that kind of pain touch El again, to make her smile, like on that birthday, always. A simple oath, impossible to uphold.

She slid onto the organ bench while El's violin scraped the stone, lifting into her arms. Where the violin came from, Len didn't ask, afraid what she might discover by scrutinizing the miracle. Cracking her knuckles, she placed her fingers on the starting keys, her feet over the pedals. "Ready?"

"Ready."

The song opened with a solo from Len. Slow, reminiscent at first. Notes twinkled from high to low, soft but always in motion, like the streams in the forest. A minute in, El joined her on the strings, and the tides shifted. The melody remained the same, but the notes were played louder and held longer, the reminiscence now a longing. They walked hand in hand through the score, serenading one another through the divide, lifting the dreary cathedral with their music.

Someone else was in the room, watching them. *This was what El had meant, wasn't it? Our mother lives through us.*

Len had taken her mother's presence for granted so long that once it fractured, she couldn't remember what it felt like. Now, she knew death was no great distance.

Notes trickled down, circling back as they wound toward the finale. The longing was once again a quiet memory, sung off their chests and ready to go back to sleep. Their fingers went limp, and silence reigned.

Her prison's shadows melted away, but a new umbrage bounced on the organ. A masked intruder perched in the goddess's now open window, swinging their legs back and forth, rolling a knife between their palms. The sound of waves once again echoed within the sanctuary, a southerly wind blowing them against the rocks, beckoning. Len reached into her gown and took hold of the gun. Running her thumb over the cold metal, she spun the chamber out, and its bullets clattered to the floor.

I won't set sail without you.

THE BRIDGE
by Courtney Chester

Lornara woke to the acrid smell of burnt flesh. A breath hitched in her throat as she surveyed the carnage left on the battlefield. Smoke still lingered over the blood-soaked grounds. Gone were the bright blue banners emblazoned with her family's crest, now burnt to ashes. Gone too, were the men who promised their lives to seat her father on a throne which did not rightly belong to him.

She twisted her wedding ring. From what she could tell, she was all that remained of her brother's army. She choked down a sob, forcing it back by biting down hard on her lip. Her mouth filled with blood; vision blurred as she fought off tears. She needed to be strong, but she was alone now. Surrounded by nothing but charred corpses. A shiver ran down her spine, spreading quickly to tremulous hands. Her chest tightened.

"Oh gods," Lornara whispered. Wymon. Her sweet, innocent little brother! The lady scrambled to her feet in a hurry and came crashing back down in the same breath. The left side of her abdomen throbbed in bitter agony. She touched the wound, blood seeping between her fingers. Grabbing a half-melted blade off the ground, she took a deep breath and pressed the metal to the laceration. She hissed and doubled over, dropping the blade.

Where was Wymon? She needed to find him. She *had* to find him. Ignoring the splitting pain in her side, she dug her hands into the ground and slowly pushed herself up to her knees. What happened here?

Then, Lornara remembered. Dragonlord Alden, her husband, atop his dreadful dragon, Caezeryn, spear at the ready. The lady remembered watching her husband launch the spear into her brother's chest. Wymon crashing to the ground. The dragon opening its smoking maw. She screamed as a torrent of fire consumed them. All incinerated in an instant. All but her.

Tears cascaded down her cheeks, carving salty trails to her lips. She twisted her wedding ring with increased fervor; it chafed, twisting the flesh of her finger, rubbing it raw. Alden knew how she loved her baby brother, how she practically raised him after their mother died in childbirth. When this mess first began, Lornara made her husband promise to let Wymon live, promise he would be pardoned for their father's crimes. And the dragonlord agreed, looked her in the eyes and swore an oath to the gods. Yet, he burned her brother alive.

"Damn him!" Lornara's scream ripped through the air, vocal cords straining against her fury. She tore off her wedding ring and flung it as far as it would fly. The lady forced herself to her feet, no longer feeling any pain. She would kill her husband herself, tearing off pieces of him she once kissed so tenderly.

She was foolish, caught up with romantic inclinations. Lornara truly believed their marriage meant something, that it would forge a true alliance, and put an end to the centuries-long feud over the throne. But her father's ambition knew no bounds and he would stop at nothing until he sat upon the throne, correcting what he deemed to be centuries of injustice. Soon, he will learn that not only he lost his chance at the throne, but his youngest son. Perhaps even, his daughter.

Lornara laughed. All this loss, for nothing at all. The lady's hand slid towards her hip where her sword lay sheathed, yet unbloodied. Alden had to be near; she was sure of it. After the destruction the dragon unleashed, Caezeryn would need to rest. Ignoring the cracking bones beneath her feet, Lornara staggered towards a bridge, the only way out of the killing fields.

* * *

As his men celebrated, the dragonlord stared off into the distance. Guilt gnawed away at his soul. He killed his brother-in-law, burned hundreds alive in an instant. Alden knew it was necessary, but he felt no satisfaction. He had not known satisfaction since the day this old, ridiculous war surged back to life, not since he had to leave his wife behind enemy lines.

Alden placed a hand into the fire pit, finding meager comfort in the warmth of the flames as they licked around his fingers. Caezeryn nestled in the far corner of the alcove, slumbering. At peace. Puffs of smoke curled gently from her snout. As he watched the fire's reflection dance across her purple scales, the dragonlord wondered what it felt like to burn, to feel his skin searing, blistering until it melted away entirely. Disturbed, he drew back his hand and stumbled backward, nearly tripping over his own feet. His men quieted, turned their attention to him.

"Ya alrigh', m'lord?" First Spear Renault asked.

Alden nodded and forced a smile back at the ginger giant of a man. Renault had always been an honorable and loyal retainer. The gesture convinced the others, who quickly returned to their drinks, but Renault lumbered towards him. The First Spear clapped a thick hand around the dragonlord's shoulder, steered him away from the others, and closer to the bridge spanning the Gold River.

"Don't let it weigh too 'eavily on you. Traitors. The lot of 'em."

"Yes …"

"Bastards! The whole lot of 'em! They wouldn't hesitate to put your brother and his wee babes to the blade." The First Spear spat onto the ground. "Anything to put their false king on the throne. Told your brother and father we should reunite those godless sava—"

"Careful," the dragonlord warned. "My wife is still of their bloodline. I will not tolerate any disrespect towards her."

Renault shook his head sadly. "My poor lad."

"What?"

"How do you think this war ends?"

Simple. It would end with Lornara's father's head on a pike as the rest of his body congealed to bile in the belly of a dragon. Most of her family will be gone, but Alden swore to himself he would stay true despite the political ramifications. But how long would they last once she discovered the truth? What he did was unforgivable. And his hoping was dependent on whether his own brother felt merciful enough to pardon Lornara.

As if sensing his fear, Renault clapped him on the back. "Yer' brother's a good king. Just have 'er prove …" he trailed off as a figure shambled onto the bridge.

"A straggler?" Alden asked.

The First Spear unsheathed his short sword, but the dragonlord stopped him as the figure came into view.

Clutching at her side, holding a sword in her right hand, Lornara stood on the bridge. Her bright, white curls were matted with filth and soot coated her face. Still, the lady's image was burned so vividly in Alden's mind he could recognize her in any form. He raced towards her, but she raised her sword as he drew near.

"I don't understand," Alden took a step back. "Darling, how are you here?"

Lornara's eyes shimmered, sweltering. "You burned him!"

"I—"

"You promised me he would be safe!"

Footsteps sounded from behind, followed by the nocking of arrows on bowstrings. "Say the word, my lord. We'll let our arrows fly," a voice announced.

Alden kept his eyes leveled on Lornara. If she was afraid, she hid it well. Her face remained a mask of ice. The lady lifted the flat of her blade against his chin, tilting back his head.

"Lower your weapons," the dragonlord ordered.

"Wha' are ya thinkin', boy?" Renault asked.

"I can handle this."

Lornara's face remained devoid of emotion as her gaze pierced through him, relentless and unyielding. "I challenge you to a duel."

Alden's men erupted into a chorus of surprise. His jaw slackened as he stared at her wide-eyed. Surely, she did not understand what she was demanding. "Lornara," Alden cautioned, voice a faint rasp. "You are in no state to fight."

"And you are in no position to make assumptions." The lady lowered her blade, but not her glare.

Alden took a step closer. "Please, this is not the way. We will find you a healer. We can put this madness behind us."

"Are you truly so craven? Only a coward would betray his own family so cruelly."

Alden stiffened. There it was. An outright accusation. He knew this would not stay secret for long, but he never imagined it would all fall apart like this. His heart hammered away in his chest. A dozen excuses flooded his mind, none of them sufficient to quell the fury he knew swelled in his wife's veins, threatening to engulf her. Just as Caezeryn's flames had her brother.

He raised his hands, a gesture of peace. "I had no choice."

A flash of silver. Then a trickle of blood down his cheek.

"Then you will have no choice but to kill me too."

He shook his head at her. "You are still my wife. No matter what has befallen—"

"Stop toying with her, lord!" his men yelled. "Kill her!"

His wife smiled. Not the warm, intimate smile he loved so. It was corrupted. Calculating. Cold. Alden knew then Lornara fully understood there was only one conclusion to their meeting on the bridge.

Lornara leaned in closer to him, close enough for him to smell the soot that clung to her hair, the smoky smell of burnt flesh. She no longer smelled like him. Like home.

"Draw your sword, husband."

Alden's hand trembled as it closed around the hilt at his side. He could hardly breathe. White-knuckled, he drew his sword, the crimson blade glinted cruelly in the moonlight, thirsty for bloodshed.

She slashed at him. He stepped back, narrowly dodging. The dragonlord countered with his own slash, an instinctual rebuttal rather than an intentional attack. The sound of steel-against-steel reverberated through the air. Alden kept striking, each one stronger than the last, forcing Lornara to backpedal. There had to be another way to end this madness, some way to end this without hurting her.

Alden ducked. His wife's sword whizzed above his head, trimming the very tips of his hair. The lady was no soldier, but he knew she trained with her brothers growing up. Not only that, but Lornara had watched every one of his sparring matches since they wed. His technique was as predictable to her as her short, hurried jabs were to him. If Alden underestimated her, she would kill him. If the dragonlord pressed too hard, he might cause irreparable damage. It was a dance, but she stumbled every other step and flourished on the next.

"I took no pleasure in it!" Alden said, breathless. "Our families are at war!"

"Wymon chose this war no more than I did. No more than you!"

"That doesn't matter!" resentment bubbled in Alden's stomach like spoiled ale. Why must she be so pig-headed? Nothing about this war had been one-sided. "My brother, your king, nearly died by your father's hand! When he woke—" Alden groaned as his wife's blade slid through the top of his shoulder.

"My father should have finished him."

It was too much, everything he felt inside. The dragonlord roared, sword raised above his head, he brought it down on her in a great arc. Lornara's sword flew from her hands, clattering to the ground. His blade took root in her left side. The lady loosened a ragged breath, staggering about.

"Lornara …" Alden stared at her, horrified. Slowly, he withdrew his blade from her and threw it behind him. Blood flowed from her waist, dripping onto the cobblestones. He caught her as she fell.

Damn it all! Alden no longer cared about his reputation or the king.

Her eyes fluttered open.

"Lornara?" he asked.

Her forehead cracked into his face.

Alden staggered backward. His nose became a fountain, heat exploded across his face. The world faded in and out.

His wife threw her weight against him, knocking him to his back. As Alden lay disoriented, Lornara positioned herself atop him, clawing at him like an alley cat. His vision cleared, and he gazed upon her face once more. Her expression was desperate, rabid. His heart ached for her, an agony worse than his shattered nose or sliced muscle. Alden seized her by the wrists, stared deeply into her amber eyes as he had a thousand times before.

"I love you."

Alden swore her face softened, that the lingering smoke above them blew away. He relaxed his grip, and her arms fell to her sides. He exhaled. Lornara cupped his cheek. Her thumb brushed over his lips gently. It was over.

She tore out the dagger he wore on his hip. He moved to grapple with her, but her other fist smashed into his face. Blinking back tears, he hissed in pain. The blade hovered above his chest. He grabbed her wrists, struggling to ward away her entire weight.

"My lord!" One of his men cried out, distracting him just for a moment.

Time slowed as Lornara wrapped another hand around his, reversing her grip on the dagger. Alden's eyes widened. The lady plunged the dagger into her own chest. Every breath Alden had fled him.

She smiled at him, satisfied. Her body slumped against his. Still. Lifeless.

Dead.

Alden sat up, shaking his head in disbelief. "No … no," he whispered over and over, cradling her body in his arms. "Lornara …"

Silence.

He stared into the night.

The dragonlord's men crowded around him, smothered him. Cheering. Whooping. Championing him as if he had accomplished something so great. As if the blood on his hands were some traitor's and not his wife's. Their words turned to distant murmurs in his ears, drowned out by the echo in his chest.

With Lornara nestled in his arms, Alden rose. Renault and the others quieted. They parted as he walked by. Curiosity marked their faces as they stared at him.

In the alcove, the campfire dwindled down to its last sparking embers. Its faint glow illuminated the sleeping dragon as Alden stood before her.

"Caezeryn," the dragonlord called.

Shaking her head, Caezeryn awoke, regarding him with a knowing gaze. She beat her wings, extinguishing the dying embers. Shrouding them in darkness.

Alden smiled, slid off his wedding band.

"My lord!" Renault shouted, panicked.

His betrayal could not be washed away, but perhaps it could burn.

FINAL OFFERING
by Maria Spence

When I got there, it took me a while to figure out how things worked. I wandered through the sterile streets and finally found my way to the town center. Scanning the square, I saw an *open* sign on a door. I squinted to read the name of the building: *Office of Reparations*. Just what I was looking for.

I marched across the square and through the door. The place was empty but for a small man dressed like he would be running numbers with his white shirt, an armband and a pencil behind his ear. Sitting at a desk, he was flipping through a stack of papers and stamping each page. I stopped in front of him and waited for him to look up. He didn't.

I cleared my throat. "I'm here to make things right. What do I do?"

Keeping his head bowed and continuing his flipping and stamping, he raised his eyes. Without a word—and continuing his flipping and stamping—he handed me a gold piece of paper with one sentence: *Write a letter and find someone to post it for you.* I raised my eyebrows in question. "Well, this seems simple," I said to the clerk. "What's the catch?"

Without a word he passed me a lavender sheet of paper. This one had a paragraph on it.

I glanced at it. "So, is this it?"

Flip. Stamp. Flip. Stamp. "Yep."

I shrugged and walked out of the building to sit on the nearest bench. I focused on the lavender paper.

Ah. You have chosen to continue. Doubtless you believe this an easy task, and it can be. But that depends on you. Your letter must be honest and accurate. It must be detailed and specific. Mostly it must seek to mend, not to justify. You will know if your letter has been read and accepted when you receive your ticket for The Train. But writing the letter is only the first step in this process. You must also find someone to post it for you. That in itself can take some time. Don't delay. All the best in your endeavor.

May you ride The Train.

That was it?

Stomping back into the empty Office of Reparations, I approached the man. Still fluidly flipping and stamping, he didn't look up but handed me a sage paper.

"What's this?" I asked, snatching it from his hand.

"Read it and you'll find out," he said, sorting the papers into piles.

Instructions for Finding Someone to Post Your Letter, was printed across the top of the page.

"Why didn't you just give this to me with the lavender paper?"

He shrugged, still not looking up from his work.

I strained to sound polite. "Are there any more papers I need?"

Still not looking up, he handed me yet another sheet of paper, a cerulean one. I exhaled loudly and took it. The top read: *Instructions for Resubmission.*

"Resubmission?" I looked at him. "What's that?"

"It's when you have to submit again."

"Yes, I can surmise that much. But why would I have to submit again?"

He finally stopped his paper shuffling and looked at me. "Because no one gets it right the first time, lady."

I held his gaze. "Well, I will."

"Good." He met my glare for a beat and went back to his stack.

"That's it? No more surprises?"

"That's it."

"Thanks!" I snapped and walked out.

Back on the bench, I looked at the sage paper.

Instructions for Finding Someone to Post Your Letter

Dear Brave Soul,

I am not surprised you chose to continue in your quest to make things right. Understand that this takes time. Do not be discouraged. Be open to learning and you will be able to complete this task.

Once you write the letter, you must find the messenger to deliver it – a vector, we call them – by nailing your letter onto the banyan tree in the town square for potential vectors to read. The one who reads your letter and grieves over it will be your vector. You will know because he or she will find you. If no vector finds you, then your letter must be revised and resubmitted.

Further instructions will be delivered – on a fuchsia piece of paper – once your vector has found you.

May you ride The Train.

Fuchsia? Really?

So where was this banyan tree? I'd only been in town a few hours, but I hadn't seen any such tree in the town center. Maybe the gentleman in the Office of Reparations would be able to give me an idea. I stood up with my rainbow of papers in my hands and turned toward the office. As I reached out to open the door, a hand flipped the sign from *open* to *closed*.

"Wait!" I knocked frantically on the glass. "Where's the banyan tree? I haven't seen anything like that in the town center!"

"You will now," he said and pulled down the shade.

"What does that mean? Don't you have a coral map to give me or something?" I yelled. Then I heard the click of the lock snapping into place.

I wasn't sure what he was paid, but whatever it was, it had to be too much. He was useless.

I turned back toward the town center, wondering how I'd ever find the tree. Deep in thought, I didn't notice where I was going but was suddenly aware of a faint floral scent in the air. I stopped. I was in front of a colossal tree with myriad branches spreading out at least thirty feet from the trunk. Many were low to the ground, but there were higher ones, reaching perhaps fifty feet into the air. The trunk was made of what looked like a group of smaller trunks with their roots stretching out from part-way up the tree. The whole thing looked like a beautiful tangle of trunks and roots stepping over each other. I had never seen anything like it. And it had most definitely not been there when I made my way to the Office of Reparations earlier in the morning. This is a tree one doesn't miss.

But there were no letters on this tree. Was it the right tree? I looked around and saw only shrubs. It had to be. The instructions had clearly said a tree, not a shrub. That Office of Reparations was empty. Maybe it was a slow time of year?

Regardless, I knew I needed to start on my letter. Back in my sparse quarters, I took a pen and piece of paper out of the desk and settled myself in to begin. I read over the instructions on the lavender paper again. I'd always had a way with words and felt confident I could do this. *My dearest sister,* I began. Soon I had a well-crafted letter in my hand. Flawless grammar and interesting, descriptive language. I expertly avoided the trite and tired in my choice of metaphor, and I knew I'd outdone myself when I read aloud the final sentence: "It is only with your forgiveness that I will ever be able to forgive myself and live the rest of my existence as a soul light enough to rise above the weight of regret and shame." And that is what I needed, a light soul. I was heavy, and heaviness did not get one on The Train.

Making my way back to the tree, I realized I had no nail and hammer to attach my letter to the tree. But it turned out my worry was unnecessary. When I arrived at the banyan tree, I saw not only a hammer and a box of nails at the tree base, but hundreds of letters hanging from the previously letter-free branches. I hadn't been gone that long. What on *Earth* was this?

I paced around the tree. Many of the letters were out of my reach, but I was able to read some. Although I hadn't seen any letters when I was there earlier, some of them seemed like they had been hanging there a long time. I looked closely at one. The writing was faded, and the paper worn, brittle. I had to look hard to read the faded words, but I could make them out.

My dearest Gillian,

I'm writing to tell you how sorry I am for everything. It seems I've wronged you, and I need to tell you I deeply regret any harm I may have caused you. I understand some things I did while we were married may have hurt you, but I never wanted to hurt you. I cherished you – just like I promised in our wedding vows – and I made you the center of my life. I took care of you and worked hard to provide for you and our kids. I know I wasn't always available, but to be fair, you weren't always available either. The children were always your obsession. When my loneliness became overwhelming, I sought solace in other places. I bought that sailboat. You liked that for a while, remember? When you didn't anymore, I found someone else who did so you could stay on land, rushing after kids and grandkids and whatever else brought you joy. And I went off on the boat with what brought me joy. Isn't that what it's all about? Finding joy? You seemed to find yours easily and I had to look a bit for mine. And I guess my

*searching hurt you. I enjoyed our life together once. I never meant to cause
you pain. I apologize from the deepest part of my soul. Please forgive me.*

Love,

Benjamin

No one would put such an old letter up here. It had to have grown
old hanging on the tree. Obviously, this letter hadn't made a vector
"grieve". I looked at the letter in my hand. Someone would surely be
moved by it before it curled and yellowed.

I grabbed the hammer and a nail and looked in earnest for a spot
to hang my own letter. I decided to try placing it next to a letter that
looked a bit fresh, instead of an older one. I came to an open area near a
letter written on clean white paper.

Daughter of my heart,

*Hello beautiful daughter. When you read this, you will no doubt be a
grown woman. Perhaps you will be old with grandchildren and a whole life
behind you. Wherever in your life you are, I want to tell you that for the rest
of my eternity, I will long to hold you. My arms have ached from emptiness
since the day I left you on the steps of the orphanage in Wanzhou. You were
sleeping, only days old. I hid you for those days, just as I hid my pregnancy.
It wasn't difficult to do. Not many people really saw me anyway. I was
invisible to the people in my village. When your mother has died in your
childhood and your father finds another wife who considers you a burden,
you learn quickly to be as small as possible.*

*I thought I had mastered the art of disappearing in a crowd until Tao.
He saw me. It was market day, and I had been sent to sell our vegetables to
the vendor so I could buy some meat and rice flour. I kept my head down as
usual, but the sound of his kind voice made me look up. "Where is Mr. Li
Jie?" I asked.*

*"He decided to expand his business to Yunyang. He's asked me to run
his stall for a while as he gets established there. I'm his nephew, Tao," he
said. His eyes were gentle. And he was tall, so tall (are you tall, precious
daughter?). So, I looked up into his face and smiled. And that was the
beginning, my lovely daughter, of what would be the best – and worst –
time of my life. It started with Tao, but it ended with me having to leave
you on the steps of the orphanage. I'm not trying to tell you that abandoning
you was good or right, or to make you feel sorry for me. When I tell you Tao
returned to his province after spending a glorious summer with me – after*

seeing me as no one had ever seen me before – having no idea he left a part of himself inside me, I don't ask that you pity me. I knew what I was doing and the risk I was taking. I knew he would never offer me marriage, but he saw me and for that I would have given much more than my virginity. For that, I did give much more. I gave you.

This letter is meant to be reparation for the wrongs I committed against you. But there's no way to repair those wrongs. Had I kept you, I am certain I would still be writing this letter to you, only asking you to forgive me for different things, that you would forgive me for giving you such a hard life – the life of an outcast, the life of one unseen. I cannot imagine the family you have now would give you such a life. So, I am not asking that you forgive me for leaving you on those steps. I'm asking you to forgive me for whatever feeling of loneliness you carry inside you. I know you carry this feeling because I carry it, too. You are a part of me, a part you will never know, but a part all the same. I have not seen you since the day I placed you carefully on the front steps, bundled warmly against the cold in a red jacket for luck, wrapped in a blanket and sleeping soundly. But I am lonely for you. You have no memory of my face. But I know you miss me, too. I know you live with some uncertainties about yourself many others do not. And you don't deserve that. You deserve security and assurance, and so much love. I hope you have at least received some of that from those you call family. It was my job to give those things to you, and I did not. Please forgive me, my beloved daughter, for not giving you those things and for leaving you to live a lifetime of not feeling whole.

It is too late, I know, to tell you this, but it is true: I love you. I even loved you when I walked away from you, tears streaming down my cold face, into the dimness of the early morning.

Love,

Your mother, Jing

I stood stunned for a moment, feeling the pain of those words that had nothing to do with me. I looked at the letter in my hand. My offenses weren't this dire. Was my letter supposed to evoke that kind of reaction? I felt a twinge of panic because I couldn't imagine it would. Best to get the nailing done before I thought too much about it.

I nailed my letter up next to the serious one. I turned to return to my quarters and stopped short. When I approached the tree with my letter, I was the only one in sight. But there, all around the tree, were people reading letters. They were all dressed in the same plain, cream-colored garments, almost like work coveralls. I could tell they were both men and women, though I couldn't explain how I knew that.

There wasn't a lot to distinguish them one from another. These must be the vectors, but where had they come from? Why hadn't I heard them arrive? And why would they all be arriving at the same time? I decided to sate my curiosity and turned to the woman closest to me.

"Hello."

She nodded at me and smiled. I was encouraged to continue. "How is it you all just arrived here?"

"Oh no," she said. "We never leave until we find the letter to make us grieve. We roam around the tree day and night, reading. We're free to go only after finding the letter we're meant to deliver."

"But you weren't here a moment ago. I didn't see any of you."

She smiled at me. "Just because you didn't see us doesn't mean we weren't here." She pointed to my letter. "You nailed a letter to the tree, so now you can see us."

"Oh!" The woman began to turn from me when I asked, "And how long have you been here reading letters?"

"That's hard to say. I think you would call it … two centuries."

"Oh, good grief! It can take that long? You mean I won't be able to get on The Train until one of you cries over my letter, and it could take *two centuries?*"

"Most people are slow to understand the task at hand, so yes, it can take a while."

I became distracted by a sudden smell of warm, brown sugar. I turned to see one of the vectors carefully reaching up in the tree, pulling down a letter. The man held the paper to his heart. He stood silently with his head bowed for what seemed a long while. When he raised his head, I saw tears on his face.

The vector smiled and nodded toward the man. "He found his letter."

"It would seem so," I said. "But how exactly do you know which letter is yours? So many of them seem sad. What makes a letter yours?"

The woman thought a moment. I suppose when you've been circling a tree for two centuries, you don't feel the need to rush much of anything. She closed her eyes and replied, "That's a difficult question. But I think the best place to start is to say there's a difference between sadness and grief. Sadness can be felt by anyone, for anyone, but grief can only be borne through experience. As we read these letters, our hearts respond to the one that somehow connects us with something in our own past, that on some level defines our own experience during our lifetime. So, while sadness is often a part of grief, they are not the same. Grief requires a mixture of self-awareness, regret, and new understanding."

Feeling a bit out of my depth, I changed the subject. "Why are some of these letters so old? Will they ever be delivered?"

"Perhaps. Those who are truly repentant usually return to the tree regularly to see if their letter has aged. But if a person is never contacted by a vector and never comes back to the banyan tree to see the condition of their letter, it can remain on the tree for a very long time, possibly forever."

"Forever? That hardly seems fair."

"Hm … I'm not sure what you deem as fair is what matters here."

Maybe she was dating the man in the Office of Reparations.

"Ma'am, I'm unsure of how things work here. I'm just trying to get my bearings," I said. "Thank you for your assistance."

As I turned to go, she said, "I read your letter."

I stopped and faced her again. "Yes, and? Will it suffice?"

She looked into my eyes and her expression became softer. "I'm not the vector meant for this letter. But I can tell you … no, I'm afraid it will only age."

"Why?" Sounding petulant even to myself, I cleared my throat and added, "What's wrong with it?"

"I can tell you suffered much at the hands of this person you wrote to—"

"My sister."

"Yes, your sister. And I am sorry that is true. But your letter does not get to the heart of what *you* need to ask forgiveness for. In fact, reading it, I'm not sure you know that. Do you?"

I should have taken offense at this question, but the way she said it—so gently, so full of compassion—I simply couldn't.

"I … I'm not sure I understand you. You read the letter. You know I didn't do anything wrong to her, at least not purposefully. What can I ask her forgiveness for?"

"And yet," the woman said, "she is the one you chose to write to. You know there is a reason. You know you must face it so you can ask her forgiveness, yes, but also so you can know and forgive yourself."

"Forgive *myself?*"

"You harbor unforgiveness toward your sister. That unforgiveness has twisted so deeply inside you, it clouds your ability to see things clearly. To see yourself clearly." She paused, and I realized I had no retort. "Take time to consider, friend. Perhaps a few amendments should be made." She smiled with those final words and walked away.

I stood as though in a dream, like a soldier who had just survived a very close explosion. Blinking slowly, I looked around me. I gave my head a little shake and watched as the vectors milled about the tree, reading. What were they looking for? Stories of repentance? Stories of forgiveness? Of both? Slowly, I made my way to a faded letter, apparently not up to snuff. What made it so wrong?

Diane,

I'm supposed to write you a letter so I can get out of this shit hole. Something about being honest and not casting blame and taking responsibility for wronging you. Damn! I think I'll head back and tell them to shove this letter up their asses, because there's nothing to take responsibility for. I didn't wrong you. I was trying to be the best father and husband and head of the family I could. But you just wouldn't get behind me. It didn't matter what I did, you couldn't put your perfect self aside and just follow. How am I supposed to lead when no one is following? What was I supposed to do? And I wronged you? I don't think so. You always thought you could lead better than me, didn't you? Did you just want me to DIE so you could take the reins? Is that it? Well, I guess you got your wish, cuz here I am. Writing this stupid letter to apologize for something that isn't my fault.

Your never-good-enough husband,

Dan

Okay, well *that* wasn't a good example. It wasn't hard to tell what *he* did wrong. Aside from being a potty-mouth, he clearly wasn't big on introspection.

"Pardon me." The voice beside me made me jump. "I didn't mean to startle you. I just need to put up my new letter."

I turned to see a man, rather on the short side, with a kind countenance and a grave look on his face.

"Sorry," I said. "I didn't hear you coming. I don't see much space in this spot here. You might have better luck someplace else on the tree."

"Oh, that's no problem. I'm replacing this one." He reached up and took down the letter I had just read.

"*You're* Dan?" I'd expected Dan to look like … well, like a selfish, angry lout instead of this simple, peaceful man.

He smiled. "You've read my letter, I see."

"Ah …" I felt a bit caught out. "Well, yes. I just did, in fact."

"Not the most impressive business, is it?"

"Um, no," I said, attempting to soften the blow, "but honest, perhaps?"

"Very," he said. "I can't say any of that is hyperbole. She didn't get behind me, and our marriage wasn't good by the end." He took a deep breath. "Equally true, I was a terrible listener." Dan looked at the new letter in his hand. "You just read my letter, so it's fresh in your mind. Can I read my new one to you?"

I didn't know this man. I had no right to hear his personal business. But hadn't I already read his first letter? And wasn't he here sharing his deepest failure with me?

Not normally the soft type, I surprised myself by gently saying: "Of course. If you'd like to read it to me, I would be honored to listen."

He smiled sadly, but with relief in his eyes.

Dear Diane,

I have had much time to consider our lives together. I remember what it was that drew me to you. While your outer beauty was what first caught my eye, it was what I saw on the inside — your strength and openness and intelligence — that made me want to stay with you. Maybe it was because I always fought feelings of inadequacy in those aspects, so I admired them in you. They seemed to come to you effortlessly, while I hid behind my sense of humor to cover up how weak and stupid I felt. You drew me out because you weren't guarded. I learned when we were together that I didn't need to be guarded either. And I loved that.

When we had children – well you know my history. You know my own parents were abusive and angry, and you know I never learned how to be vulnerable in that relationship. And parenting just seemed to expose my feelings of never measuring up. But you always knew what to do. And you always knowing just made my never knowing more obvious. As our kids got older, I realized they saw that too, and I turned to what was easy. I turned to anger and alcohol. I blamed you for turning the kids against me and for ruining my relationship with them. What I really wanted was to be able to be like you. Instead, I hated myself for the fact that I wasn't.

I cannot change anything, Diane. I cannot undo my past. But I have taken this time to look deep into myself and see that what I did to you and our children was wrong. I do love you. I always have. But you could never know that because my love was hidden under layers of garbage. I'm cleaning house. I hope you can forgive me.

With love and humility,

Daniel

My eyes stung as Dan looked at me. "I don't know what the vectors are looking for, but I think you're a lot closer this time."

"I hope so," he said. "But even if I'm not completely there yet, I feel right. I feel truthful for the first time in a long time."

"How did you get to this point? This letter couldn't be more different than the first."

"Actually, this is my fourth," he said, hanging his new letter.

"What? You mean you wrote something even worse?"

"Well, that all depends on what you consider *worse*. My first letter basically said nothing. I evaded the issue, denied I ever had a problem. Just asked for some general forgiveness for not being the best husband I could be. After that one turned brown, I tried again. That time, I wrote all about my growing up and how awful my parents were. I spent the whole letter blaming them for everything and never got around to doing much apologizing. By the time I wrote that letter you read, I'd had it. I was tired of being here, of feeling worthless. I just vomited on the page. It was angry, but it was truthful. At least, more truthful than I'd been before. I knew it wasn't an apology. I knew it wouldn't get chosen by a vector. I went back to my quarters and spent time with my arms crossed, feeling justified for my venom in that letter. Then my eye lighted on the paper with the instructions—"

"The lavender one?"

"Just the one." He nodded. "I re-read the paragraph, and it made sense to me like it hadn't before. '*You must write a letter that honestly and accurately addresses the situation … it must seek to mend, not to justify.*' I hadn't followed the instructions. I was still hiding behind my pride and fear. My goal hadn't been mending at all, but casting blame. Yet the blame lay with me, at least, in large part."

"That must have been a hard realization."

"Very. I can't tell you the depth of shame I felt for so long. I would have come sooner had it not been so."

"What finally happened to make you come now?"

"I had a visitor. The man from the Office of Reparations."

"What? How on Earth could he help you? Heaven knows customer service isn't his strong suit."

Dan smiled. "It wasn't him so much as what he brought. He brought me this letter." He pulled out an envelope from his jacket pocket and handed it to me.

"You want me to read it?" I felt horribly intrusive, despite my curiosity.

"I'm happy to share with you. It was written for me, of course, so it may not say what you need to hear, but it was just what I needed to finish my latest draft." He saw me hesitate. "Go ahead, read it."

I took the envelope from his hand and removed the letter.

Hello Dan.

I see you have come to an important part of your journey. You have stepped into honesty. Very good. Honesty is not always easy, or attractive. It rarely shines a light on something to show it as all good or all bad. It is messy. But no one moves on to ride The Train without it. It takes courage. Let me remind you of some truths you once knew. Your sins are forgiven. Pick up your mat and walk. You no longer need to be paralyzed by your past and your failures. If you let go of your right to anger, your right to withhold forgiveness from others and from yourself, you can walk into this next phase of eternity – or rather, ride into this next phase. That's one truth. Yet another is that redemption is real. Nothing and no one are beyond that when they step into Truth, because the truth sets you free. Meditate on these words. See what new insights they bring. Keep working toward riding The Train and do not fear. Only the brave can ride The Train.

I look forward to welcoming you soon,

The Conductor

"The Conductor?" I said. "Well, there is a train, so I guess it makes sense, but … who's that?"

"Surely you know The Conductor." Dan's face became bright with his large smile. "It's because of him we are even here."

"It is? What do you mean? I've never met a conductor."

"Yes, I can see how you might think that. Honestly, it took me a while to understand his role in this process. What I know is that before you were called to do this work of reparations, you were called by The Conductor. You just didn't call him that."

I thought about the words The Conductor had written to Dan. I'd heard them before. Yes, perhaps I did know The Conductor.

"So, will I also get a letter from this Conductor?"

"Possibly. If you need encouragement in truth and the courage to face what's in your heart. His words began to work their way into my thoughts. After some time, I was able to sit down and pen my latest letter. Since I did that, I have felt at peace." We were both silent for a moment, then he said, "I've taken an awful lot of your time. Thank you for talking with me."

"You've helped me so much, I—"

Just then, a warm breeze and the scent of roses rushed past us, and I heard a gentle cry. I looked round and saw a vector holding Dan's letter and gazing at it with what seemed a mixture of love and pain. Dan saw him too.

"Hello," Dan said. "That's my letter. Will you deliver it for me?"

The man turned to look at Dan. "I will," he said, smiling as tears filled his eyes. His voice sounded like velvet, full and warm. "This is beautiful, and painful. I pray she will hear you."

Dan nodded.

That's right. The cerulean paper had said the letter had to be read *and* accepted.

"Excuse me," I said, "how do people in the living world receive our letters? How do you post them?"

"The most common is in a dream," the vector replied in his rich voice, "but it is not always possible. Insomnia makes dreams unavailable to us. Alcohol or drugs make sleeping minds inaccessible to vectors. So, we have other ways." He nodded as if to say this was as much information as I would get.

A sudden apprehension seized me. "Do you deliver to those no longer in the living world?"

He smiled. "They're much easier to deliver to."

Of course they would be, I thought, and breathed a sigh of relief. "Thank you. I also have a letter on the tree. I was told I may need to amend it."

"Yes, it is often so. We have found that is part of the process. Don't be afraid to go through it." He turned to Dan. "I must go now. Dan, I am proud to post your letter." He took a fuchsia paper (the fuchsia paper!) from his pocket and handed it to Dan. "May you ride The Train." He bowed to Dan and left.

We stood staring after him. I missed his voice already.

"Congratulations, Dan," I said. "I hope to follow your lead. What does the fuchsia paper say?"

He looked down at the paper. "I think it is just for me,"

"Oh," I said, embarrassed. "That's okay. It's time I went back to rewrite my letter. Thank you for all you shared with me. I think I understand better what I need to do."

"I'm so glad." Dan smiled. "May you ride The Train."

I nodded and turned to go back to where I had hung my own letter, next to the sad and serious one. When I found my letter again, I was astonished to see it had already begun to brown on the edges. I reached up to pull it down, but try as I might, I couldn't loosen it.

"That won't do you any good, love." A gruff Scottish lilt sounded beside me.

I turned to see a small woman with short gray hair and a deeply lined face.

Feeling panicked by the state of my letter I asked: "Why is my letter so old? I just nailed it here a bit ago. And why can't I get it down now?"

"Won't do to take it down 'fore you have another to replace it. As for why it looks old, I dunna think time here is like what you're used to." She winked.

"Of course," I said. I noticed the sad and serious letter was gone. That had to mean a vector took it. Relief flooded through me. I couldn't help but feel that Jing didn't deserve to wait centuries for her letter to be delivered. She'd waited a lifetime already.

"Best to read your letter over from where y'are and head back to write a fresh one as soon as ya can. I'm here for the same thing. Wrote to my da. But I missed the mark. Need to try again." With that, she walked around the tree in search of her own letter.

"The process is the process," I said to myself and turned to re-read my letter. Still grammatically flawless, I could see now there was no heart in it, no real ownership of my own failure. I thought of Jing's letter, so full of anguish but casting no blame—not even on the man who left her pregnant. She owned what she chose, boldly declared both her situation, which was beyond her control, and her own choices, which were within it. She called it the tragedy it was and held herself accountable for her role in it.

Only the brave can ride The Train. Jing showed what it meant to be brave.

Walking back to my quarters, snatches of the last few hours (years?) raced through my mind. Dan told me I knew The Conductor. I agreed he was right. But I also felt certain that I wasn't there to see him.

Lines from my failed letter to my sister floated in my mind. I thought of Dan's letter from the Conductor. What had it said? *If you let go of your right to anger, your right to withhold forgiveness from others and from yourself* ... How did my asking for her forgiveness equate to my forgiving myself?

Sitting at the small desk in my quarters, I took out a fresh piece of white paper, closed my eyes and exhaled slowly.

"Conductor," I said, "I know you can hear me. I know you're waiting for me to board The Train, and you will wait until I'm ready. Until I get this right. Thank you for that kindness. I am about to write to my sister again. Will you guide my thoughts, and show me the truth behind the lies I have always believed?"

I can't be sure how long I wrote. The resulting letter was not long, but the words were slow to come, like a thick rope being pulled through a horribly narrow tube. I felt the words scrape against my soul, rough truths rubbing the walls of the lies I had built, the justifications erected to enable myself to be okay with my choices. As I pulled the rope, writing down notions I had never allowed myself to entertain, I could feel the tautness of the truth as I named it and owned it, and finally, the release of that tension as I confessed my need for forgiveness. I could sense the approach of the peace I so desperately wanted.

My trip back to the banyan tree was contemplative. My mind was filled with memories from my life. Early on, I accepted that all the goodness in the world couldn't make me righteous. We all fall short, some by a little, some by a lot, but short is short. There was still a gap between what was required and what we were able to do on our own. We needed a way back to our Creator. And He provided it. When I was alive, I knew of a certain birth, of a life and death. Then, of a resurrection. Here, I learned of The Conductor. In my heart of hearts, I knew they were one and the same.

I stood before the tree with my letter. Reaching up to grab my now very old letter, faded and frayed around the edges. I took hold of it and paused to read it one last time.

My dearest sister,

You and I have always been very different people. We saw every aspect of life from our own perspective. From marriage to parenting, to business to friendships, there was rarely a topic we could see eye-to-eye on, and that made it very hard for us to connect. You often reacted as a wounded animal might, lashing out for fear of someone hurting you further. You sought to control every situation so you would not be a victim of someone else's control. I never desired control over you. I simply didn't want you to control me. If you were a wounded animal, I was more like the waters of an ocean, pulled far out to sea before being dashed on a distant beach, constantly thrust onward by the desire for a life of significance. So, I went. And that was part of the problem, the distance I created. I hurt you by making my life separate from yours. You never forgave me for that, and I so wish you would. It is only with your forgiveness that I will ever be able to forgive myself and live the rest of my existence as a soul light enough to rise above the weight of regret and shame.

Sincerely,

Marianne

Grimacing, I tore the old letter down and nailed up the new one. This letter was closer to the truth. I had no idea if it would make a vector grieve, but it was honest. I had asked for the Conductor's help, and he had given it.

After only taking a few steps away from the tree, I heard an exclamation and smelled the heady scent of jasmine. I turned back and saw a woman holding my letter, tears falling down her cheeks. "I would be honored to deliver your letter," the vector said. I nodded, my eyes locked on hers, and she surprised me by saying, "May I read it aloud to you so you can hear the beauty in it that I do?" Her voice was honey, sweet and medicinal. Somehow, I knew I needed to hear my words in that voice.

"Yes. Please," I said quietly. I closed my eyes as her melodic voice began:

Dear Jo,

I want to tell you I'm here in this "God-forsaken place," because that is something I would say. But today I realized it isn't God-forsaken. God is very much here. Moreover, he's giving me the opportunity to make things right with you. So here I am. I want you to know I've spent many years telling myself I did nothing wrong in our relationship – not because I was perfect, but because of all the wrong that I laid at your feet. You ran me off by making every event about you. And truly, you did make everything about you, that is, not run me off. Running was entirely my own doing. I convinced myself I was taking the "high road," because it meant I was not yelling back at you. I have had to dig deep to understand what it is I need to ask your forgiveness for. But I realized my choice to cut myself off from you wasn't about taking the moral high ground. It was a way to avoid telling you the truth – the truth about how I felt, yes, but also the truth that you really needed to hear. We were given to each other as sisters to sharpen each other. Who else in your life should be able to go toe to toe with you if not one with the same fiery blood in her veins? Instead, I left you to navigate the world without someone to understand you, someone to tell you to get your head out and to love you as you fought to do that. My own emotional safety took center stage. You never learned that love never fails, because I failed you. I missed the purpose of family, the gift in the struggle. Please forgive me, Jo, for being selfish and cowardly. Please forgive me for not fighting for what we should have had, even if that meant fighting with you.

With much love and regret,

Marianne

The sudden intensity of the silence when she stopped reading pressed in on me. It surrounded me, cushioned me, caressed me. It was like I was feeling an embrace, wonderful, comforting. I felt light, as though I had taken off a pack filled with stones. I opened my wet eyes.

My vector was gone. My letter was gone, and in its place was my fuchsia paper. I reached up and took it off the tree. I looked around to see if anyone was watching me. I seemed to be alone, though I knew I wasn't. It was just what I needed at that moment: solitude to read this final note. I leaned my back against the massive trunk of the banyan and opened my letter.

Marianne,

You have carried the weight of this failed relationship throughout your life. You could not know the magnitude of its defining power in your life, the way shame and guilt colored everything you believed about yourself, and everything you believed about me. Of all the people in your life, this relationship is largely what defined who you became. That is why you had to write to Jo.

Long ago, I became your Conductor, so you have always had a ticket for The Train waiting for you. The question was never if, but when you would ride. You are about to spend all eternity living as a fragrant offering to the Father. This place is your final opportunity to "leave your gift at the altar and make things right with your brother" so you can do that. And you did. I'm proud of you, but more than that, I'm glad for you that you no longer must carry this weight.

There is one last thing you need to do before you board The Train.

You have asked for forgiveness.

Now you must give it.

I turned the page over and caught my breath. I knew that handwriting.

Dear Marianne,

I'm sure you're already enjoying heaven. This has taken me so long to get right, and I'm not even sure if it is right this time. But somehow, it feels more right.

I could hear her voice as I read, hear the slight irritation always in her tone, the impatience. And some resignation, too. It had been so long since I'd heard her. She died so much younger than she should have. Tears came easily.

I've tried every way possible to get out of blaming myself for what happened between us. In life, it was easy to convince myself you were nothing but a selfish, uncaring person. I honestly believed that most of the time. I spent so much of my life feeling lonely. My two marriages didn't fix that. My six kids didn't fix that. Holding tightly to our mother didn't fix that. And you, well you weren't around enough to remedy my emptiness, either. When we were growing up, I had such high hopes we would be friends someday. I watched you have plenty of friends. I was just never one of them.

If I'm being honest, I know I can't blame you for not wanting to be around me. I was depressed and said some awful things. People do that when they are so consumed with their own hurt, they can't see anyone else's. I never thought you had any hurt. I know now everyone has hurt, no matter how things look from the outside. Over the years, I built my walls so I wouldn't need you. And I didn't. Until the end, when I did. And there you were. My beautiful sister. You were still bossy and thought you knew it all, but that's what I needed, someone to take care of things. I'm sorry I didn't value that before, Marianne. I'm sorry it took being in the final stages of brain cancer for me to let go of all my resentments toward you. I didn't feel I had a sister all my life, but I made sure you didn't either. Can you forgive me?

Your sister,

Jo

Holding tightly to the letter, I closed my eyes as sobs wracked my body. She had never apologized to me for anything, ever. We wasted so much time. Oh, Jo. I took a deep breath and whispered, "Yes, Jo. I forgive you. I always wanted to."

I opened my eyes to find I was no longer at the banyan tree. I was on the platform of a train station.

"I'm waiting for the train," I said in wonder.

"So am I," said someone next to me. I knew that voice.

I turned.

"Jo?"

"You know it is." She was young again, beautiful as she had been when she was twenty, before she had stopped taking care of herself. Before anger and resentment put a permanent scowl on her face. Before cancer. I couldn't stop staring at her.

"But how can you be here? You died so much sooner than I did. You've been here the whole time?"

She smiled. "Either I'm a slow learner … or I was meant to wait for you." Jo looked full into my eyes, so much love there I could hardly stand it. "I don't mind."

A wave of gratitude swept over me. I felt so humbled. "Thank you," I said. "I love you, Jo."

"I love you too." She reached out and pulled me into an embrace. Sweet tranquility settled over me as I held her. I don't remember the last time we hugged, but this was what I imagined it could feel like.

Just then, I heard a train approaching and pulled away suddenly.

"The Train! I don't have my ticket!"

"I'm your ticket," Jo said. "I know you're mine." She grabbed my hand as the Train pulled to a stop and the doors slid open. We looked at each other and she gestured toward the open door. "Shall we?"

Together, we stepped in.

Shepherd

By Lee Patton

"Do you understand what I am asking of you, Mical?" Azra said, his amber eyes glowing in the pale moonlight spilling through the window of an otherwise dark room. The fire had long since succumbed to the ravages of time, ousted by the passage of long hours.

Mical sat in silence, pondering the question. His gray eyes fixed on the smoldering ashes in the fireplace. The dull red light of the embers brightened, dimmed, then faded away. Mical could not help but mourn. For what little warmth remained, he would never know it again.

After a moment, Mical returned Azra's gaze. "What is the Hour of the Harvest?"

"It is a time hidden within time. It passes unseen and unfelt by all but you and me, allowing us to perform our task unhindered."

"That task being the Harvest."

"Yes."

Mical shuddered as a chill crept across the surface of his skin. "But why do you need me? You have been doing this forever. Are you not eternal?"

Azra smiled. He looked out the window, watching the crescent moon drift across the night sky, near the renewal of its phase. "I need you because you are sensitive to the Hour. Aware of it. To say that it was *you* who found me would be closer to the truth. The Shepherd is chosen, but not by us. We are merely drawn to the next when our time has come."

Azra turned his gaze back to Mical, continued: "No, we are not eternal. Though we perform our task for eons, all things must come to an end. Even us."

Mical breathed deeply and looked back to the fireplace, desiring the return of the fire. Of the heat. The light.

"Can I refuse?"

"No."

The darkness remained. Azra stood, making his way to the window. Mical followed, taking a place beside him and listened to the sigh of the wind passing through the boughs of the trees. "Will I go around covered in a black sheet carrying a scythe?"

A chuckle escaped Azra. "Of course not. I would, however, recommend a suit. It is good to keep a professional appearance. Out of respect."

"Respect for what?"

"For the souls that you will collect. For the souls that you will guide," Azra motioned to a gray case resting upon the table by the window. "As for your tools," he reached into the case, "you will need only these."

He held a small book, covered in aged black leather, and a black pen. "During the Hour, you will be drawn to those souls who must depart from this world. You only need to write their names here in the *Kiniga Zhizni*, the Book of Life, and their souls will vacate their bodies. Those souls will rest within the case until you deliver them safely to the Judge."

"The Judge?"

"Yes. The Judge is the one who determines the ultimate fate of the souls you carry."

"What is he like?"

"You will understand when you meet Him. No explanation I could give would do Him justice."

Mical's fingertips brushed against the book. He hesitated, then took the book and pen. "I have to admit, this all seems overly simplistic."

"Death is not complicated, Mical. No, the trouble is always what happens afterwards."

"What do you mean?"

Azra sighed, running a hand through his pitch-black hair. "The Hour does not belong only to us. Evil spirits haunt the realm of the dead, searching for the souls you carry, to devour them. And you."

Mical's eyes widened. "What am I supposed to do?" he said, stepping back.

"You fight. Your role as the Shepherd is not only to guide, but also to protect."

"How? With what?"

Azra took the book. "Click the pen, three times, quickly."

A look of confusion spread over Mical's face as he did so. The pen glowed with an ethereal light, extending in length and curving at the end so that he had to hold it with both hands. The light faded to reveal a large scythe. Its blade rang with a song of requiem, a dread chorus calling the wicked to oblivion.

Mical's eyes blazed with fury, his body surged with power. Azra stepped forward, ran his hand along the length of the blade. It returned to its former shape, a pen resting in Mical's hand.

"This is the *Pesnya Smyerti*. The Song of Death. Now, do you understand what I am asking of you?"

Mical nodded, his fingers closing around the pen. It was cold. Heavy.

"Then it is time," Azra said, opening the book and laying it on the table.

"Time for what?"

"For you to write my name."

Mical shook his head. "What?"

"The first soul each Shepherd claims is the one who came before."

"Why?"

"To teach you your first and most important lesson."

"What is it?"

"That even death may die."

JUST BEFORE DUSK
By Frank William Finney

I followed the elves
to the pyrite gate

while trolls from the fields
passed a flask around

and an ogre from the wood
lit a blazing bonfire.

I sat and watched
from the riverbank

while a faun with a limp
toasted marshmallows.

To the Watcher on the Tower
By James D. Mills

Another hot day, not even a whisper of wind, nor wisp of cloud. The sky was clear, blue, and so god-damned overwhelming. The only relief came from the occasional airship floating by overhead, blotting out the sun for a few short minutes. Reyna was sweating, had been since a quarter past the eighth bell. The twelfth bell just rang, which meant eight more until her watch was over. After, she would descend a hundred hot iron rungs, grab a drink at Marne's, then do it all again the next morning.

Simple. Easy. That was all Reyna wanted out of life.

Today was anything but. Some days were like that. Engineering students gathered at the quay in front of the customs building, protesting the recent book bannings.

Commander Gellus warned Reyna that morning it might happen. "Be prepared to fire if things get out of hand."

Reyna enlisted in the watch years ago and had yet to fire her weapon on duty. There had never been a need to. High Rock was a peaceful city, kept safe by the great Sorcerous Kings who built it for the newly arrived humans. Few of her comrades had fired on anyone while on duty; only five watchers of a thousand. Three of them did so on the same day.

On weekends, Reyna's troupe gathered at the Undercity shooting range not far from where she grew up—before the humans appeared. Each watcher was issued a large bore rifle equipped with a telescopic sight capable of taking down a bison at 250 meters with a single shot. One shot was all they got. It was all the rifles could hold.

Reyna heard tell of an updated design with an increased capacity for ammunition, but the Division of Ethical Technological Advancement shut it down, long ago. Too much power in the hands of those not naturally inclined to wield it. If an incident called for more force to resolve it, there were always fire dancers on standby for crowd control. Thankfully, Reyna had never seen them at work.

Reyna watched the students roiling below, blowing trumpets, beating on drums and chanting something she could not make out from atop her watchtower. Almost every student was human, and not one possessed a sorcerous bone in their body. The gift was not meant for them.

Her trigger finger itched, and Reyna found herself tapping against the barrel of her rifle, listening to the echo reverberating through the chamber to touch a ball of lead, waiting to taste burning flesh. She forced herself to stop. Commander Gellus would have her in the pillory if he caught her doing that. The likelihood of a misfire was almost zero, but the crack of a gunshot could turn a protest into a riot. And riots meant fire dancers.

No one wanted that.

Instead, Reyna took to picking at a gray sliver of dead skin from her thumb with one hand, using the other to hold the rifle steady. She often grew restless up on the tower, especially when it was so hot, the sun bearing down on her. The Teyomi were not meant to be above ground. Not during the day, at least. Another aspect of her culture that had been altered by the humans.

One late night at Marne's, Reyna was drinking with Sergeant Hennin, whom she grew up with in the Undercity. He had indulged in one too many, and when he leaned over to whisper in her ear, she thought he was coming on to her. She wished it had been that simple.

"You know we're only up here because the Sorcerers want to keep them under control, right?" Hennin said. "I mean, it's bloody obvious!"

No, Reyna had not known that, nor would she have come to such a conclusion on her own. She resented his casual libel of the good Sorcerous Kings, those who had brought an end to the chaos of her mother's youth. They built High Rock for the humans so they could live as they were accustomed; in the open, under the sun.

Hennin's words wormed their way into Reyna's head, repeating as she lay in bed that night, and every night hence, as she forced herself to sleep at an unnatural time for the sake of the greater good. The Kings were benevolent. They saved her people from certain doom. "But here we are," she mouthed, staring up at the ceiling. "Here we are, circling them on all sides. A cage for animals."

Below, the drums and trumpets ceased, replaced with bitter shouts. Reyna snapped her rifle into position, looked through the scope to see what was happening. Aegis enforcers were in a line pushing into the mass of students, beating them with cudgels.

This was when her job became difficult. She had one shot, and a long reload. Targets must be high value, with the line of fire clear of innocents. Reyna's shot had to put an end to chaos. There could be no mistakes. But there were hundreds of students down there, humans and Teyomi alike.

"They were chanting," Reyna whispered. "They were just chanting."

She looked over to Hennin's tower, then to Gellus'. Neither one had yet fired, so she would follow suit. It was protocol for an officer to open fire first, and then for subordinates to follow with a volley. It prevented mistakes.

Chanting turned to yelling, screaming, and Reyna saw yellow clouds of smoke bloom from the crowd. Some of the students began to disperse, fleeing before what came next. The enforcers advanced. She saw they now held maces and swords. Shots would soon be fired; fire dancers would be released. All hell would break loose.

"Enough!" A booming voice roared over the crowd. A robed man stood at the top of the stairs to the customs building. A Sorcerous King, manifesting in person. Reyna could see him in her crosshairs. Such an appearance was unheard of.

All went quiet, aside from scattered coughing and sputtering wails of pain. Then someone shouted, and the protest erupted into a riot. The thunder of gunfire exploded all round. Reyna raised her rifle. She had one shot to end the chaos.

THE VALUE OF HORNS
by James Callan

When it comes to trolls, horns are paramount to one's identity. More than a badge of status, they transcend mere ornamentation. For trolls, size matters—the bigger the better—especially when it comes to their horns. Although, the shape, curve, twist, and hue are no less important than the length and girth. Troll horns are versatile, multifaceted in their purpose. They are used for combat, for attracting mates, for intimidation and glamour. Horns are at the center of troll fashion and, in some tribes, even of great spiritual significance. For trolls, be they of the cave or forest or mountain clans, horns are everything. And so, it begs the question: what is a troll without horns?

Is he truly a troll at all?

Gromby asks himself this question each day. *What am I? Am I truly a troll?* He rubs at his hornless head and feels a smooth scalp beneath coarse, tousled hair. It is a habit he developed, a constant reminder of his dire lack. Without the slightest of nubs to suggest that maybe, just maybe, his horns might be coming in, he mourns for the missing hallmarks of a troll. And so, when going about Trollgate, Gromby has taken to wearing a cap.

Grimdolyn, widely known among the clans as the most beautiful troll of all, possesses ashen horns, slender, and deadly-sharp. Rising from the edges of her dragon-bone tiara, keratin spires sprout out of her gray-gold hair. They shine in the sun, shimmer in the moon, and dance with amber light in the evening bonfires and troll-hall hearths. Grimdolyn is the envy of many a maiden troll, and the center of many a man-troll's lust.

From afar—or near, if he is lucky—Gromby admires Grimdolyn's prodigious nose, how it slopes upward between her crimson eyes to meet at the roots of her celestial horns, as lovely and grand as twin ivory towers.

Borgoth the Mighty, who is rough around the edges and wide around the waist, is famed for his slaying of the dreaded undead dragon, Skullhorn, a feat of extraordinary heroics accomplished in his youth. Well-seasoned, if not yet old, Borgoth is no longer the warrior he once was. Even so, his name carries weight, his past deeds, clout, and is respected throughout the clans, by warrior, layman, and priest. His horns are thick and curved, spiraling inward at his temples, hard and heavy as anvils. He has split the skull of many a ram, risking his own in provoking their furious, headlong charges.

At the center of Trollgate, in the town square, Borgoth's burly visage is etched into the conical monument that stands as tall as any ogre; the single horn of Skullhorn, which has since been dubbed Skysplitter.

Now gazing up at Skysplitter from beneath the cap that covers his hornless head, Gromby considers, not for the first time, how discriminating the gods can be with the gifts they bestow, and to whom they are given. He rubs at his unadorned pate, staring into the graven eyes of Borgoth the Mighty. Someone sighs in admiration, a swoon of sorts, and Gromby rolls his eyes, annoyed to discover Grimdolyn standing nearby while gazing longingly up at the hero's monument. Despite his irritation, his outright jealousy for Borgoth, Gromby withers when Grimdolyn lowers her gaze to meet his own, dismantled by her disarming beauty.

"Is he not the bravest, most dashing, most noble of trolls in all of Trollgate, nay, in all the clans, to the furthest reaches of the world?" Grimdolyn muses as she twirls a lock of hair around a finger no less fair.

Gromby is enchanted by the scarlet sparkle in Grimdolyn's eyes, by her charm, which is rendered intoxicating by the love she feels for the famed troll Gromby himself wishes he could be. He would do anything to appease Grimdolyn. Sighing, he lowers his head. "It is as you say, Lady Grimdolyn. There is no doubting it: Borgoth the Mighty is the finest troll among us, across mountain, forest, and cave."

Grimdolyn titters, a coy eruption. "And such *big* horns…"

Gromby reaches under his cap to rub his head. "Yes." He swallows his pride. "Such very big horns."

* * *

When Borgoth the Mighty was wedded to Grimdolyn the Fair, Gromby the Hornless reflected, not for the last time, how discriminating the gods can be with the gifts they bestow, and to whom. With enough bitterness to fill the hollow of Skysplitter, Gromby considered the harsh truth of it all: unless a troll is uncommonly privileged, one would waste much time awaiting the capricious goodwill of the gods. And so, not wishing to play the luckless fool any longer, Gromby turns his back on them, both the spiteful gods and the privileged trolls whom they favor. It would be naive to sit and wait for fortune to sprout out of his head from nothing.

This is his conviction.

He might not have horns on his head, but he has a fine brain within it. It is time he put it to use.

* * *

They want horns. I'll give them horns!

These words became Gromby's mantra, echoing across the numerous lands where his quest to procure distinguished horns of value guided him.

They want horns. I'll give them horns!

Each syllable is tinged with chagrin, imbued with a strong, resentful sentiment fueling Gromby's newfound ambition to become the horniest troll in Trollgate, in all the world. If he could not grow horns from his head like a normal troll, well, he would seek them out on his own, collecting them from a menagerie of horned beasts. Where undead dragons failed to surface from the ancient crypts of the lithosphere— and well outside the bounds of his capability to slay one, even if they had—Gromby relied on other rare and mythical creatures to cross his path, animals with horns of peculiar magnificence.

Days turned into weeks, weeks into months. Seasons came and went, passing in a haze. Before Gromby realized it, years had gone by, as many to comprise a decade.

Gromby had not intended to be gone for so long. Even so, he could not deny the worth of his labor. His collection grew vast, more impressive than any he surmised existed in all the world. He often recollected his journey with satisfaction, his catalogue of horns, with pride.

There was the fabled golden yak, its mammoth horns bearing a fine, gilded gleam. Gromby paid an ogre to brain the beast. And that was that. One less living link to a myth. Then there was the chimera, which Gromby tracked for many weeks, and slayed with poisoned arrows. It was a poor shot. One to the rump. The poison spread slowly through the monster. Eventually it died… days later. During the many weeks of tracking the chimera, and his eventual slaying of the magical animal, Gromby had not considered in the end he would be rewarded with mere goat horns, bearing nothing to distinguish them from the typical kind. No evidence showed they came from the head of a goat joined with the body of a ferocious lion. It was not Gromby's finest moment.

More precious by far than any of his other acquisitions, perhaps more than all the other horns combined, was the alicorn that Gromby severed from a living unicorn, a black mare of extreme rarity.

It is an evil deed to maim a unicorn, a taboo far beyond the moral compass of most sentient beings.

Gromby was hardly ignorant of these well-known facts. However, his own moral compass had become warped, skewed by his desperate desire for the world's finest horns, to have them for himself in place of the gods' cruel neglect of his natural birthright. When he at last severed the alicorn clean from the most magical being in all the realms, he did so without an ounce of remorse.

And Gromby continued his merciless hunt.

Minotaur horns, satyr horns, demon horns—so many horns. When the mythical and magical eluded Gromby, he turned to common beasts: oryx, oxen, and rhino. In the end, he acquired more horns than he could carry.

Though they were not his natural horns, they were his horns nonetheless, horns owned *by* him, and he had managed to graft many of them to his body using arcane methods of witchcraft. At long last, Gromby was a horned troll. More than that, he was uniquely outfitted, and there were none, not even Borgoth the Mighty, who could rival his fine accoutrements.

The time had arrived. Gromby returned home to Trollgate.

* * *

Gromby's homecoming was meant to be sweet, a victory and mighty boast, a proclamation to all those doubting that Gromby was now truly great, a mighty horned troll. But the gods are fickle at best, and even Borgoth the Mighty may fall from their favor. It would be no great surprise if they were to abandon Gromby once again as they did from the start.

Trollgate looms ahead, and as Gromby struts into his hometown for the first time in ten long years, he finds himself robbed of any chance to show off his horned and elevated self. He is astounded to discover his home in ruins; Trollgate razed to scattered husks of scorched stone. Lying among the tussled thatch roofing and blankets of fresh snow are countless troll bodies. They clog the wide roads of the town square and the narrow avenues between ransacked homes. Some bodies are whole, others dismembered, torn limb from limb.

Some look to have been burned, while others, face down in water, were likely drowned. Whoever killed the trolls of Trollgate was inconsistent in their savage methods of murder, but there is one consistent feature among the dead: there is not a single troll left with its horns upon its head.

"Who goes there?" The voice is rough, coarse as wyvern hide. A man steps out from the shadows, his mailed fist clutching a thick lock of gray-gold hair. His free arm is wrapped around two objects, twin spirals, slender, graceful, and white as bone. They are beautiful, and Gromby seems to recall these horns from long ago. Then it becomes clear. He recognizes the way they gleam, so intense and bright, even under the gloom of a somber overcast.

"Grimdolyn …" Her name is a breath of remorse, a longing for a troll woman he never truly knew. It escapes Gromby's lips in a tattered gauze of mist, dispersing into nothing, vanishing as a specter.

"Grimdolyn, was it?" The man encumbered with Grimdolyn's horns drops them into the snow and mud. The blade of his sword rings in the silence as the armored man pulls it free from his scabbard. "You trolls have the ugliest names, you know that?" He laughs long, loud, and more cruelly than Gromby has ever heard a man laugh. "The horns, on the other hand," the man continues, "well, those are rather pretty."

Sword drawn, the man takes a step towards Gromby, revealing a wagon behind him. The wagon's loaded cache of bones—no, horns—troll horns, are stacked as high as Skysplitter, which sits in a second wagon, secured by rope.

"They fetch a fine price, troll horns. Your hides, too, but your horns most of all." The man's grin is wicked, his biting blade caked with blood. "Aye, you got some nice horns there yourself. Very unusual. Very valuable, no doubt."

Gromby rubs his head, fingering the base of the alicorn magically fused to his skull. He rubs at the satyr horns that sprout from behind his ears. "What, these horns?" He staggers back a step. "These horns aren't mine. They're just ornamentation. Nothing more. I have no horns. Never have."

The man lowers his sword, leers at Gromby, studying him for a moment before laughing as he did before. "You trolls are stupid things," he says as he spits into the snow. "But you know something? You're good for a laugh, and you're even better for your horns."

"No, really, they aren't mine. I swear, I'm hornless! Gromby the Hornless. That's what they call me. Gromby the Hornless!"

"Well, Gromby the Hornless," the man takes up his sword once more, "they won't be calling you anything no more." He gestures with his sword at the bodies scattered in every direction. "*They* are all dead. But don't worry, Gromby the Hornless. You'll see them again."

The man removes his gauntlet and places his dirty fingers into his mouth, a shrill whistle piercing the frozen air. From behind the ruins of burnt troll halls and homes emerge several figures, dozens of humans, armed men with blood on their shields and horns in their arms.

"We missed one, boys." The man points at Gromby. "With horns the likes of which I've never seen."

The mass of marauders piles in on Gromby, hold him down, and take up their knives to carve free his precious horns.

"No! I swear! They're not mine! I have no horns! I am Gromby the Hornless. Hornless, I tell you!"

One of the men shakes his head, takes out his fire-blackened dagger and sets it to the base of Gromby's horns. "Shut up and hold still. It'll all be over in a minute."

"Mercy! Mercy!"

"Come now," the man chides. "You can't blame us for what we've done here. We're only human, and you wouldn't believe the value of these horns."

Gromby opens his mouth, but his protests lodge in his throat, choked by pain. His vision goes red as he tastes iron. Gromby, once more, is Hornless.

#849   OLD TROLL

AHOY THERE!
by John Mueter

It was calm out on the open ocean, hardly a breath of wind. Adrian was grateful for that. He sat cross-legged in a fiberglass dinghy, a poor vessel to be sailing if the seas turned rough. Sensible or not, it was the boat provided by the brilliant Dr. Vijay Ramachandra, an endearingly eccentric genius who ran a clandestine time-travel operation from his university office. Well, to be exact, his house, but with heavy borrowings of university assets, especially in terms of personnel. He had been sending individuals, staff and students, into the past for years now.

Exploring the future held no interest for the professor. "If you want to go to Alderaan," he would say, when the subject came up, "get in touch with Luke Skywalker."

It occurred to Adrian, gliding along in his glorified rowboat, that Ramachandra may have been careless in his planning. The professor was a bit barmy to begin with. Everybody knew that. If this little excursion didn't go according to plan, Adrian would be stuck up the creek without a paddle, figuratively speaking, in the middle of the friggin' Indian Ocean hundreds of miles off the coast of India, in a flimsy rowboat. But the professor had often proven his prowess in prognostication.

Adrian had learned to trust it. And he did. Until this moment, anyway.

His own previous "launch", back to 1765 France, had been straightforward. He was re-incorporated in a field near a road outside of Rouen, as planned, and in five minutes the promised carriage had arrived. The only qualification he possessed for that gig was he knew some French. The rest did not go well—but that's another story.

Adrian was surprised to be asked to go on this present launch, albeit as a second choice, filling in for someone who had backed out at the last minute. He didn't blame the designated traveler for getting cold feet. Everyone who knew about Rama's secret program was aware that, in the previous year, one of the travelers never returned from ancient Rome. That was not a propitious sign.

Maybe he was assassinated in the Senate House? Ha! I'll permit myself some dark humor, mused Adrian, who had been rowing vigorously the whole time. Giving up on that, he placed the oars back in the boat and stretched out his long legs as best he could. The dinghy was not built for a 6'3" person. He massaged his knees, the undulations of the water rocking the boat with a gentle rhythm. Closing his eyes, Adrian's thoughts turned back to the prodigious professor.

After Rama had verified the time and location, there was no stopping the launch; it had to take place. Adrian could not fathom how the professor was able to see into a specific point in the past and predict what was about to happen. Rama declared he wanted to try something different this time by transporting an object as well, in this instance, the dinghy. He had purchased the used boat from a private owner who, he admitted, seemed a bit shady. Adrian felt like a laboratory monkey being launched into outer space in a homemade rocket.

Adrian removed his jacket, wiping his brow with the sleeve of his shirt. The early morning sun was growing hotter by the minute. *If that damn tub doesn't show up soon, I'll be a hard-boiled egg,* he reflected, rearranging his cramped legs. He would have the questionable luxury of contemplating these matters until the promised ship turned up.

That is, if it did at all.

Squinting, he scoured the horizon to the west. There was something out there, a small object—and it was moving! It had to be the three-masted barque, the *Aberdeen*. What a fine sight it was to behold. *Three cheers for Rama, who got it right yet again!*

Adrian breathed a sigh of relief. That relief, however, was short lived.

Unfortunately, there hadn't been an opportunity for him to properly prepare for this blast to the past, and his grasp of European history was dodgy. He was a grad student in sociology, not history. It was June of 1853, that much he'd been told, along with a few other basic facts about the ship soon to pick him up, like the names of the ship and her captain.

Adrian struggled to remember what was going on in the world in the middle of the nineteenth century. Victoria was on the throne in England, and Albert was her consort—that much he knew for sure. Still, he had some time yet to consider the history before the *Aberdeen* drew near.

Nearly an hour later, he was relieved to see the ship slowing down as it approached. Adrian stood, waving his arms even though he was sure he had been seen. If nothing else, it gave him a chance to exercise his limbs. Then, he braced himself for the inevitable awkward first meeting. How would he explain himself? First, there was the problematic fact of his being a time traveler, as well as the unlikely circumstance of his being adrift in a dinghy in the middle of the ocean.

He realized he should have given the details concerning his situation more thought.

Rama didn't seem to have given them much thought either. Too late now. The *Aberdeen* had decreased her speed considerably, having reefed nearly all her sails. A skiff was being lowered from the side. Adrian could see many spectators at the gunwales, what must have been the entire crew of the *Aberdeen* and her passengers, no doubt curious about the spectacle of a flimsy boat with a single individual inside.

"Ahoy there!" he yelled; a gesture as superfluous as waving his arms had been.

"Sir! Are you quite alright?" asked one of the sailors in the approaching skiff, apparently, the one in charge. He had expected to discover a half-starved wreck of a man, dying of thirst. He was astonished to find a young lad, bright as a penny, clean shaven, neatly dressed, exhibiting no distress whatsoever.

"I'm fine, thank you. I'll be even better once we're aboard the ship." He didn't want to provide any further explanations, as he knew he would have to repeat them all over again anyway.

"Climb in, sir, and do watch your step." The sailor helped Adrian aboard, then gave the dinghy a once over, puzzled by the look of it. It didn't seem to be made of any sort of recognizable material. He attached a rope to the bow and tied the other end to the aft of the skiff.

The short distance to the *Aberdeen* passed quickly. Adrian felt conspicuous sitting in the bow, and the rowers eyed him with suspicion. He had attempted to dress in as neutral a style as he could—a simple, light jacket, a plain white shirt, blue cotton pants—but he must have looked outlandish anyway. Maybe the Converse high-tops weren't the best choice after all. And the Polo Ralph Lauren logo on the shirt pocket, and . . . too many details that must have stuck out like a Rolex watch on a flop house hobo.

The *Aberdeen* was a British vessel, a merchant and passenger ship in service to the East India Company. He climbed the rope ladder up the side without difficulty, having been an Eagle Scout not so many years ago. He gave a crisp salute but immediately regretted having done so. After all, this was not a military vessel, not a "ship of the line". And he was no sailor. The captain, surrounded by the other officers, a bevy of gaping seamen and passengers, ignored his gaffe. Adrian towered over everybody. He must have seemed a giant. People back then were much smaller in stature.

"How do you do, Captain Fenwick," Adrian blurted without thinking. He regretted that too, as soon as he mentioned the name. If Adrian's appearance and size had not been enough cause for the captain to be shocked, the fact that a total stranger fished out of the middle of the ocean could know his name, left Fenwick momentarily speechless. He slowly took Adrian's offered hand, looking him over from head to foot.

"How do you do, sir?" Fenwick began, stammering. "Welcome aboard. May I ask your name—and how do you happen to know mine? How did you come to be drifting out here?"

"I'm Adrian Connor, from the United States of America. So happy to meet you. It's a long story, trust me. I was beginning to fry under that hot sun. Could I bother you for something to drink?" He looked around, as if expecting to find the pool-side bar open for business.

Fenwick was taken aback at the brusqueness and casual manner of the stranger, but he kept his composure. The man was clearly an American, and quite young. That would explain a lot. "Of course. Indeed, I am all anticipation to hear your story. Please, join me in my cabin."

* * *

They were alone in the captain's quarters except for Bobrick, his steward. It was a small but well-lit room at the stern of the ship. Captain Fenwick, his well-trimmed beard streaked with a touch of grey, took a seat and indicated that Adrian should do likewise.

Fenwick looked at the steward. "Bobrick, bring us some barley water and a pot of tea."

Bobrick was not eager to leave the room. He was as curious as anyone else aboard the ship to hear the story of the mysterious passenger. He ambled toward the exit *molto lento*.

Fenwick sat upright in his chair, not at all relaxed. He was a seasoned ship's captain and not one to be easily rattled. Yet, the stranger's physical appearance and manner, not to mention his strange origin, all made him uneasy.

"So, Mr. Connor, once again, let me welcome you aboard. I must say that, in all my years at sea, I have never come across a situation such as this—an individual drifting alone in a craft not very seaworthy with no provisions, no distress . . . well, how might that be explained? I am even more astonished that you would know my name, as though you were expecting the *Aberdeen* to come sailing over the horizon." He looked at his guest intently, inviting him to respond.

"That you came 'sailing over the horizon' was a bit of good luck, was it not?" Adrian said. Fenwick laughed uncomfortably. Adrian had decided that telling the truth, that he was a time traveler, was too outlandish a fact to reveal. He would need to invent some other explanation.

"First of all, I'm very grateful to you for rescuing me. The ocean is a huge place for such a small boat." The captain nodded in agreement. "Where to begin . . ." Adrian looked up at the ceiling, as if he could find an answer there. "I was vacationing in Sindh, after a visit to the Punjab. Several days ago, I boarded a pleasure boat in Karachi, one owned by a wealthy businessman, a friend of a friend. We planned to cruise for a few days and then return to the port."

"A pleasure boat?" inquired the captain. "What kind of ship is that? I have never heard of such an excursion being organized in India."

"Well, it was. That's all I can say." Adrian couldn't explain further as he knew little of mid-nineteenth century sailing ships in India. He did know that the Raj, British India, included what is now Pakistan and Afghanistan, so Karachi was a feasible point of departure. And Karachi was in Sindh province. At least he got that right.

Adrian's brain went into overdrive: "On the third night out we were rammed, hit by an unknown force—a whale, perhaps? The ship capsized. Apparently, I'm the only survivor." It all sounded a bit ridiculous, even to him.

The captain was silent as Bobrick returned with the refreshments. He set them on the table and turned to leave, once again, indolently shuffling to the door.

Fenwick waited until the steward exited the room. "That is quite an extraordinary account, Mr. Connor. You are the only survivor? How then did you manage to get into the dinghy? And I have never heard of whales swimming these waters, not to mention ramming a larger vessel. They are not aggressive creatures unless provoked." He paused, looking puzzled. "Of course, there is the matter of you being familiar with my name. Kindly explain that to me."

This was indeed a tough question. Beads of sweat appeared on Adrian's brow, this time not from the heat. He had to come up with something plausible.

"Oh, that," he said, shifting in his seat. "I was looking through a list of current sailing vessels in the service of the East India Company and must have come across your name."

"Really?" Fenwick asked, incredulously. "You came across my name and remembered it? Why, there are hundreds of vessels in the service of the E.I.C. And there are an equal number of captains! How is it that you could recall my name?"

"I have photographic memory."

"You have a photo—what?"

Oops! thought Adrian. Of course, the term is unknown. Photography has barely been invented.

"I . . . er . . . have the capacity to commit entire pages to memory. It's an odd talent." Adrian fervently hoped that the captain would not test it further.

"Odd? I'll say it is," Fenwick commented. He didn't know what to make of this stranger, a collection of improbabilities and oddments. And what was he wearing on his feet?

From the skeptical look on Fenwick's face, Adrian could tell he wasn't buying it. Captain Fenwick had treated him well so far and was worthy of respect. He felt ashamed and decided to come clean.

Lowering his head, he spoke more softly. "I'm sorry, Captain Fenwick, but I haven't been entirely honest with you. Not honest at all, actually." He sighed, sinking into his chair. "You deserve to hear the truth. But that story is even more improbable than the one I just told you. I wasn't on a pleasure cruise and there was no accident. The ship didn't sink." He paused here, unsure how to proceed.

"Well? I am waiting for your explanation." Fenwick leaned forward.

"The truth is, believe it or not, I'm a time traveler." Adrian paused to let this sink in. "I've come from the beginning of the twenty-first century, the year 2024, in fact. That's, let me see, 167 years in the future."

There was a long silence. Fenwick looked as if he had just been sideswiped by an errant boom in a gale.

At last, he spoke, quietly and deliberately. "Mr. Connor, I don't know if I've brought a lunatic on board or not. You're a 'time traveler' you say? I certainly have never heard of such a thing. I will need to consider this for a while. In the meantime, it is best, I think, that we do not share this information with anyone else. Are you in agreement?"

"Yes. Yes, of course." Adrian was relieved the captain hadn't ordered him thrown overboard. "Do have a look at my dinghy. It's also from the future and made from a material called fiberglass. That should bolster my claim, I think."

I hope, Adrian thought to himself.

Captain Fenwick continued, "Well, we shall not dwell on this any further. You are welcome to stay aboard the *Aberdeen* until we arrive in Bombay, four days from now. We can find some appropriate accommodation for you as a guest. There is nearly a full complement of passengers on board. However, Mr. Thomas Torville is occupying a double cabin. I am sure he would not mind the company. I believe you will enjoy meeting him. Now for tea. Please, tell me more about yourself, Mr. Connor."

Fenwick poured the tea.

Adrian told him that he was a student, enrolled in a prestigious university in the state of Connecticut, studying sociology, a term he had to explain. He went on to say that he visited India once before and wanted to see it in the nineteenth century as well. Fenwick raised his eyebrows at that. It seemed he was not yet ready to explore Adrian's time travel. When they finished drinking their tea, Fenwick stood up and gave a slight bow, indicating the interview was at an end.

"Bobrick will show you to your cabin, Mr. Connor. Until later." As soon as he turned, Bobrick came in.

No doubt, he had been listening at the door.

* * *

Thomas Torville was pleasant enough—friendly, talkative, but not too inquisitive. A dealer in textiles, he was on his way to Allahabad to purchase stock for his Liverpool firm, Lauren & Boss, Ltd. The cabin was cramped, though furnished only with bunk beds, a writing table, and a small chair. As Adrian had no baggage, there was no unpacking to do.

Tom, as he preferred to be addressed, appeared puzzled at first by Adrian's appearance but made no comment. "Welcome to the ship, old man. Let's take you up on deck and show you the glories of the *Aberdeen*," he said, with a smile. "Although there really isn't much to see. No end of water, of course!" He laughed heartily at his own feeble wit. "And you will want to meet the other passengers. I know they are eager to meet you."

On the deck, Adrian was introduced to each of the passengers. They were civil enough and very curious about him, but too polite to ask any questions. The crew cast sideways glances his way. Soon, lunch was announced, and everyone descended below deck to the dining room.

Some of the crew had remained on deck examining the curious vessel the new passenger had arrived in. Hauled up out of the water, it was deposited at the stern of the ship, ironically situated just above the captain's quarters, where Adrian had spun his absurd tales. Indeed, the dinghy was not made of wood, but of some unknown material, strong and inexplicably light. One man alone could pick it up. What kind of wood was this? And what were these near weightless oars made of? Some sort of metal, to be sure, but nothing these men had ever encountered.

Their curiosity slowly turned to incredulity. One of the men pointed out that the name of the craft was *Little Devil*, neatly lettered on each side of the prow. Still more scandalous, they discovered the figure of a female painted on the stern, an alluring, bare-breasted mermaid with flowing, golden blond hair and flashing a lascivious grin. There was a collective gasp.

"It's a creature of the devil," muttered one of the older seamen as he crossed himself.

Sailors are notoriously superstitious. This lot was no exception.

* * *

Twelve were at lunch. Captain Fenwick excused himself, with regrets, to the passengers. Conversation began with remarks about the quality of the repast which, after so many weeks at sea, grew dull and tedious. The comments grew tedious as well. Eventually, one of the party addressed Adrian, inquiring about his origins.

Mrs. Ethel Crapston-Bigge introduced herself and her husband. She was an ample woman, swathed in yards of drab brown muslin, with an unmistakably imperious air. Her husband, the Reverend Samuel Crapston-Bigge, was a frail, sickly man, content to sit in silence.

"Mr. Connor—do I have the name right?—how does it happen that a person of your young age is able to travel the world?"

Adrian was again put on the spot, having to improvise and weave a web of fantasies. He had a wealthy aunt, he explained, who provided him with the means to support such travel. That much was not entirely untrue.

"And why do you come to India, of all places?" she pressed further, putting down her fork and focusing a penetrating gaze on him. "You could go to Rome or Paris. Don't young American men prefer to dally there? Spending evenings at the *Moulin Rouge,* ogling chorus girls dancing the cancan and such?"

"Now, now," interjected Tom, who was fed up with the woman's dour attitude, having endured her disagreeable comments for too many weeks already. "Just because he is a young American doesn't mean he is dissolute. And how do you even know of the *Moulin Rouge?*"

"I know plenty about the vile ways of the world, Mr. Torville, more than I care to," she retorted.

Adrian was surprised to hear this unamiable exchange and chose to ignore it. "I'm fascinated with Indian culture and want to explore the marvelous places I have read about, especially the temples and the exotic landscapes. And one *must* experience the Taj Mahal, don't you agree? I've even dabbled in studying Sanskrit."

"Learning Sanskrit? Whatever for? It is the language of a backward and barbarous culture. Are you acquainted with suttee, Mr. Connor, the ritual where widows are expected to fling themselves onto the lit funeral pyres of their departed spouses? Well, what do you say to that?"

"That's only one small aspect of Indian life. The country has an ancient culture offering many wonders. There is a lot more to India than that bizarre practice. Besides, suttee has been legally outlawed." His studies in sociology came in handy after all.

"That may be the case, but what good has it done? Those Indians are stuck in their primitive ways." She glared at him disapprovingly. "We are on our way to India, returning for the third time, to our mission in Hyderabad," she went on, "so that we may continue converting the heathens from their idolatrous ways. For the wonders you speak of are the works of Satan. All those idols and the impenetrable hocus pocus . . ." She broke off and huffed disdainfully.

"Other cultures have much to teach us," countered Adrian, attempting to soften the tone of the conversation.

"I wonder if you are even a Christian, speaking like that."

"Well, I was actually brought up as a Methodist, but I ditched the whole business as soon as I could."

"And there we have it!" she proclaimed, banging a hand on the table. "So, you're a Godless atheist! I suspected as much."

With that the subject was closed. Adrian was astonished at the blatant ignorance and prejudice of the woman. He had read about people like her, and seen them portrayed in films, but actually meeting one was a bit of a shock. This was the Victorian missionary mentality come to life.

Silence fell upon the company like a wet blanket.

Adrian's thoughts wandered and he could hardly suppress a smile when they turned to the reigning monarch, Queen Victoria, and the rumor that circulated even then that the Royal Consort Prince Albert sported a rather scandalous piercing. He imagined asking Mrs. Crapston-Bigge if she knew what it was, and then having to explain it to her. What euphémismes would he employ referring to a certain body part of the Royal Prince, all but unmentionable for Victorian sensibilities: his banana? his plonker? his chopper? *Surely, she wouldn't know what a schlong was*, he thought.

And with that absurdity he inadvertently laughed out loud.

"You find this amusing, do you?" She was working herself into a lather. "We are bringing salvation to the heathen masses of the subcontinent of India, and you see fit to laugh!"

"Oh no, I wasn't laughing at that, I was thinking of . . ."

She plowed on indignantly, "Well, with your strange dress and permissive attitudes, we can only wonder if you yourself are not an instrument of the Devil." With that she rose from her chair and flung her napkin onto her plate. "You are not fit company for any Christian, Mr. Connor. Come along, Samuel."

The poor Reverend left his place at the table, his meal only half-eaten, and meekly followed her out of the dining room. If she only knew what Adrian had actually been thinking about . . .

Mr. Torville broke the ensuing tension caused by the unexpected and rather dramatic departure of the couple: "I say, the old bat knows how to make a scene!"

* * *

Bobrick, who loved to gossip, had indeed been listening at the door of the captain's quarters during his interview with Adrian. Having heard only muffled pieces of the conversation, his imagination filled in what he missed. And what he subsequently reported to the crew and passengers was the exaggerated, muddled concoction of an over-active mind. The crew members who inspected the dinghy, in turn, spread the notion that the stranger, plucked out of the sea just hours earlier, was a bringer of bad luck—the most ominous epithet in their nautical lexicon.

Captain Fenwick soon heard all these opinions, some whispered in hushed tones, and they disturbed him greatly. The last thing any captain wants is restiveness on his ship, a mood that can all too easily get out of hand. Fenwick was a peaceful man, and he strove above all else to run a happy ship.

Mrs. Crapston-Bigge came to him first, vociferously protesting the presence of Adrian Connor aboard the *Aberdeen*, then the Second Officer, nervously presenting the conclusions of the deck crew that the stranger's presence was bad luck for the ship. It was no help at all that Adrian had made such an alarming account of himself.

A time traveler—just what the hell was that anyway? Thought the captain.

* * *

After lunch, Adrian returned to the main deck. He remained alone at the gunwale, eschewed by everyone, passengers and crew alike. The sea was still calm, vast and empty. Captain Fenwick approached him and immediately cut to the chase.

"Mr. Connor, I am sorry to say that I will have to renege on my offer to let you stay aboard the *Aberdeen*. The passengers and crew are in an uproar, and I cannot tolerate that on my ship. I regret to tell you this, but I am putting you back in your boat and removing you from my ship." He paused for a moment, observing Adrian with pity. "I do not know who you really are or where you are from. Frankly, I can make no sense of this whole episode. I will furnish you with some provisions, enough to last a few days. Perhaps you can make it to wherever you are sailing. I wish you well." Captain Fenwick offered his hand and Adrian shook it, not entirely surprised by this turn of events.

The captain's words were the last anyone would speak to him aboard the ship.

The *Little Devil* was lowered into the water. The crew scowled as Adrian climbed down the rope ladder. He seated himself as before. The aluminum oars were in place. Everyone watched silently from the gunwales as the dinghy drifted away from the *Aberdeen*. There were no goodbyes, only a half-hearted wave from Tom Torville. Mrs. Ethel Crapston-Bigge turned her back to him.

* * *

A brass band and colored streamers would have been a nice gesture, mused Adrian. He wasn't awfully put out by his removal from the ship. It was awkward and unpleasant to be banished, but it wasn't catastrophic. He had options. Adrian activated the special device, another of Ramachandra's inventions, which was safely secured on a chain around his neck. It sent the signal that he was ready to return.

He hoped that Rama would be able to find him and transport him back to the twenty-first century before too long. Rowing to Bombay was not an appealing prospect. If there was one distinction in this whole sorry affair, it was this had been the shortest launch into the past in the entire history of Ramachandra's time travel experiments. He had been on board he *Aberdeen* for only a few hours.

Drifting in the solitude of the sea, Adrian ruminated on his recent experience. He was amused at the thought of Mrs. Ethel Crapston-Bigge. He could imagine her as the matron of a women's penitentiary for the incorrigible, or as the abbess of a secluded convent dedicated to the Order of the Sisters of Perpetual Misery. It made him laugh out loud to imagine her being flung off a cliff onto a blazing funeral pyre.

Take that, Mrs. Big Crap! A fit of uncontrollable mirth overcame him. He laughed at the ridiculous woman, at himself for attempting to pass off such a ludicrous story to Captain Fenwick, at his absurd predicament, that he was all alone and helpless in the middle of nowhere.

Adrian settled in and stretched out his legs, once again attempting to make himself as comfortable as possible. He gazed towards the east, watching as the *Aberdeen* gradually sunk beneath the horizon. A slight but refreshing breeze came up from the north. Adrian Connor breathed deeply, taking in the fresh ocean air.

There was nothing else to do now but wait.

SEA'S ELEGY
by Aubrey Zahn

The sea was scorched sludge beneath the broiling sky. Jess sought refuge in the captain's quarters, her cabin—once elegant, long since fallen to ruin—and could still feel the sun's searing fingers seeking her, probing through wooden slats in a relentless, baleful blaze. *Stranded, utterly alone.* The thought rolled over her like a tidal wave. Collapsing into her chair, its aching legs groaning under the strain, the captain ran sickly fingers through her grease matted hair.

Many days past, disease had begun to spread in the festering heat after the ship was becalmed on the turgid waters. Desiccated and dwindling, the crew hauled their dead overboard until at last, only Jess and Michael remained. Michael died two days ago. Jess found him crisping like an upturned beetle on the deck near the bow, and no longer possessed even the strength to heave his shriveled body over the gunwale. And so, the captain left him there, a forsaken figurehead, a testament to her failure.

Jess knew their quest had been a fool's errand.

Twenty years after the Collapse, a rumor emerged. Survivors whispered of a colony, deep in the Arctic Circle, which had escaped the rest of the world's devastation, where not only humans, but also plants and animals were thriving, and not merely clinging to life. *Was it enough to stake their lives on?* The captain often wondered after hearing of the boreal haven. *Not likely.* But what else remained to them other than to die in the burning anguish of the south? It was but a faint hope, a mirage, which drove her small crew northward over the rancid, turbid seas.

With trembling hands, Jess unlocked the desk drawer and retrieved her revolver. She estimated she had a day, maybe two, before heat and thirst took her. There was no prize for needless suffering.

In the shadows of the drawer, the metal felt cool in her hand. Jess held it gently against her cheek, relishing its unexpected chill. The captain took a deep breath, pressed the muzzle to her temple.

"Captain?"

A man stood in the doorway. Jess noticed at once that he looked... healthy. His curly hair was thick, lustrous; his brown skin had a wholesome glow, unlike her own withered flesh. He was dressed simply in a soft cotton shirt and grey trousers.

"Yes?" Jess replied, laying the pistol on the desk.

He is not real.

The hallucinations had begun yesterday. But those had been formless shades, umbral blurs at the edge of her vision, urgent voices calling her name. Nothing this substantial had yet attempted to lay claim to her mind. *Perhaps this is what happens near the end.*

"I'm Colson," he said, revealing a beautiful smile.

Eyes wide, cheeks suddenly flushed, Jess stared for a moment, then shifted in her chair, glancing at the pistol. "Jessica Mallorn," she replied, added wryly, "if you've come for my soul, you arrived just in time." Colson lingered in the doorway. "You may come in, though I don't know who, or what, you are."

Colson approached, sat opposite her. There was no weight to him, but he carried a faint scent, something clean and herbal. "A seafaring spirit," he said. "We travel the routes we sailed in life. Sometimes we spot a… compatriot from out of time and stop to see them off."

As sensible an explanation as any other, I suppose.

"Welcome to the end of the world," Jess said, waving a feeble arm towards the porthole. Her parched throat stung. She had not spoken aloud since Michael died.

"May I?" Colson asked, reaching for her face. "I want to show you something."

Jess nodded, unsure as to what she was assenting, too exhausted to care.

The spirit placed his ephemeral hand on Jess' fevered brow.

She gasped as she was transported from the stifling cabin, now standing on the deck of a strange ship. A crisp breeze, smelling of salt and fresh rainwater, filled the sails billowing overhead. The captain breathed deeply and stared in wonder at the water. The sea was azure crystal, sunlight glimmering in the crests of tranquil waves. Clouds meandered across the sky, some violet and heavy with rain, others white and wispy. In the distance were verdant mounds that took a moment to register as land. *Is it possible those are* all *trees?* Nearby, several large creatures with sleek, gray skin leapt from the water, their staccato chirping filling the air, before diving back under the waves.

Colson's gaze held the horizon. "The seas I once sailed."

Jess turned to the sound of his voice and found herself back in the cabin, dazed, slammed into her dying body on her dead ship. She slumped forward, nauseated.

After a moment, Jess looked at the spirit, asked: "How long ago was it? Your time?"

Pre-Collapse, surely. But for the seas to be that clear and blue, it must have been centuries ago, before the eutrophication and acidification of the oceans, before the currents failed and the ice caps melted.

"Linear time is for the living," Colson said, his voice cryptic, "but I'm not from your past."

"What?" Jess sat up, heart fluttering in her chest.

"Yours was a dark time in history. I'm sorry you had to live through it and die before seeing it end." Colson's expression was pitying, but the joy flooding Jess was boundless.

"The seas aren't dead," she whispered, hardly able to speak. "It doesn't last forever."

Colson's eyes widened. "No, did you think—"

"I thought it was hopeless."

"You should know better, seafarer. All waves have peaks and troughs." Colson's voice grew faint.

Is he vanishing, or am I?

Jess looked out the porthole, saw the same rotting sea, deepening from brown to murky black as the crimson sun set. Even if the fabled arctic colony existed, it seemed almost impossible for the planet to recover from this.

Almost.

Jess closed her eyes, felt his caress on her cheek. It felt like rain.

JOURNEY TO THE FERTILE LAND
by Alicia Alves

I shift into my human form to adjust the twigs in my woven basket. It will serve as my bed for the night, as well as my vessel to carry meager supplies during the day. The twigs are sharp and overused. There is no point in gathering new ones, since the trees are all dead and dry. It would make no difference to my comfort.

Once the nest is perfected, I climb a nearby tree to place it on a higher branch closer to the trunk where it is somewhat obscured. The bare branches are poor coverage for my home. But it is still safer to sleep in a tree as a crow than to sleep on the ground as a human. I don't have much food, but the bit of dried meat I do have is certainly worth killing for.

Humans may try to kill me as a bird for the meat I would provide, but it is easier to escape with my wings. Humans cannot reach me in the air. It is the one place I feel free, where my empty belly allows me to fly even higher, even if my wings are still almost too weak to carry my weight. In the air, I am that much less human, and I revel in it.

I grew up in this land, my village all too close to human villages. Once, skirmishes were common between our peoples. They hated us because they feared our difference, and we hated them because of their brutality. Truthfully, the famine pushed us to steal from each other, and tensions only grew as both groups gave in to their hunger. Skirmishes turned to battles, and battles turned to war between the nations, and the land had been salted to ensure my people could never grow crops again.

I can still hear the screams of my people. The shrieks of those who had not been able to shift in time. They haunt my dreams as I huddle in my hidden nest.

"Seek the Fertile Land, my darling," my mother whispered to me as she died that day. I could not speak as the only water I had flowed from my eyes. I held onto her as the life fled her body. My sister fell beside her in our home, and I already saw my father's body through the open door. He was slumped across the threshold, died defending our home from invaders. I alone hid beneath creaking floorboards as the humans broke through and my family died defending what was ours.

The Fertile Land was a myth, a fairy tale told to children to give them hope, and I doubted its existence. Still, I whispered my promise, "I will, Mama."

For her, for my fallen family, I would search for this Promised Land. I took what little food remained in the cellar the pillaging humans missed, and I set out on my journey.

No matter where I went, I was met with dry, useless earth and no crops. The woven basket I carry on my back now only barely weighs me down. The twigs are heavier than what they carry. I consume the crumbs within, but it is not enough. For now, sleep must be my sustenance, though it is fitful and full of memories of those I have lost, it is also filled by my promise. I must keep searching.

In the morning, I stay in my crow form, and I pick up my nest with sharp talons and fly high. This way, I can cover more ground more quickly. I am too hungry to walk to the Fertile Land. So, I struggle against the wind and the weight of the twigs, and carry on as always.

Flying above the humans, I have heard tales of the Fertile Land. I suppose the story has spread far and wide. Before the humans attacked our village, I thought it was only a story among my people. Now, I know better. Now, I know the Fertile Land is dangerous and worth killing for. And yet, it is the only chance I have for survival, and the only reason I continue to open my eyes in the morning.

Flying above the humans these past months, listening to their stories, I learned how I might find the Fertile Land. And so, I fly, swallowing any hope rising in my breast to feed my hunger. I must keep going, even though I doubt the Fertile Land exists. At least, I have direction.

A glint in my peripheral vision makes my heart flutter and I land. I can never resist found treasures, and I could use the rest. I tire so quickly from flight these days. I stand in a farmer's field, but the soil is barren, and the barns are abandoned. Still, I am careful as I walk across the field. The grass crunches under my feet and dissolves into dust to mix with the dry dirt, my talons slip through decaying leaves. The glint was from a broken, gold bracelet. There is barely enough shine left on it for me to have seen from the sky, but the sun still found enough polish to reflect its rays. Gold is useless now and often discarded.

I pick it up with my beak and add it to my basket. With so little food to be found, these treasures are the only things I collect. In my human form, I wear my treasures as jewelry or ornaments on my otherwise simple clothing, including twigs and pinecones, but my favorite ornaments are anything reflective. This way, I shine in the sunlight too. I look fondly at the gold. It was worth the danger.

The farmhouse stands menacingly, wood rotted and punched with holes to the darkness within. The darkness beckons me, and I hop closer to it. There may be something abandoned inside. A hidden cellar or an animal who perished within those walls, not yet been found. I reach the edge of the shadows when a face appears in the gap between wooden boards.

"Hey!" a man shouts, and soon the sneering, drooling face is joined by three others with similar features. "Get it, boys!"

I hesitate, tempted to fight them for the possibility of food, but there are too many of them and I am too weak. So, I take my basket and flee.

I leap into the air where the men cannot follow.

"Come back here!" they scream, and I feel a whoosh of air near my right wing as one of them throws a pointed stick at me. I dodge it easily. They are, after all, just as weak and hungry as I am. But still, I glance below to make sure I am out of their reach.

One man falls to his knees and weeps, and the others watch me longingly. I fear their hunger, but I understand it. Their hunger is my hunger. I leave the farmhouse behind, along with any treasures within its walls. I squawk my forgiveness to the men who chased me. We are all hungry in this world, and I cannot fault them for taking any food they can find.

After a couple of hours of alternating flight with rest, I spy another house, just as dilapidated as the farmhouse. I circle it a few times before landing, my previous encounter making me more cautious, but then I notice a bowl of apples on the front porch below. Juicy, red apples. At least half a dozen of them. It is too easy, and yet I must try, even if it is a trap. I must take the chance.

I land onto the porch and shift. I reach out with human hands and barely feel the skin of the fruit before plunging it between my teeth to bite. A heavy, dull taste fills my mouth, and something thick coats my teeth. I spit out the fruit, and only then realized what my brain was too slow to comprehend. The apple is wax. Laughter flows from inside the house. A child points at me from behind the glass and looks at a woman beside him. She is laughing too.

I throw the apple at the window, and they jump. I swallow the wax to have something to fill my belly. I shift, gather my basket in my talons, and take to the skies.

"Stupid bird," the child shrieks into the air. I hear the chorus of it as mother and child scream at my retreating form. Again, I look to make sure their weapons cannot reach me, but they are unarmed. The child reaches up and stretches his fingers as though he can catch me, and his lips open and close as though he is smacking them before a meal.

"Stupid bird, stupid bird, stupid bird!"

I fly higher, letting the rushing wind drown out their cries and dry my tears. So close. So close to a morsel to calm this hunger. Yes, I am a stupid bird to think I could find food so easily. I knew it was a trap, and still I went. Will the Fertile Land be the same? Perhaps it has already been taken, a trap for all to follow. Perhaps I will only find death there. If it even exists at all.

The sky is never-ending blue on the horizon, and the ground below is an infinity of dull brown, useless earth. I fear I will fly forever. My trembling wings are too tired to carry me any farther, and I start to descend. I am about to give up on finding the Fertile Land. Give up on my promise.

But then, in the distance, there is a speck of green on the horizon. It grows larger as I glide towards it. Could it be? No… It must be a mirage, another trap. I open my talons and let my basket fall to the earth. These things no longer matter. If this is the Fertile Land, I will make it there or die trying.

My wings shake and the wind almost knocks me down, but I carry on.

Below, I hear shouting and clanging metal. I look down and see blurred human forms collide, so small from my vantage point I cannot differentiate one human from another as a battle rages beneath me.

Two sides fighting over the Fertile Land beyond. It is a small circle of vibrant green pressed against deadness. It is a beacon, and I push past the pain in my muscles to reach it, though I fear I will drop dead before I can. There are no second chances, there is no rest. I must go now if I want to live.

I hold my breath as I fly over the fighting figures below, and I watch for any bows pointed in my direction. But the humans are too focused on each other to notice me flying so high above them. Why waste an arrow on one bird when such bounty lies so close?

I close my eyes and soar over the battle until I feel the air grow cool above lush, living trees. I open my eyes and descend into the shade of this promised haven.

At last, my feet touch soft earth. I shift and feel clean air enter my human lungs. I grab the closest apple, and delight in the crisp bite of it, the sound is sustenance to my starved ears. The flesh of the apple is sweet and juicy, and the wetness on my cracked lips and chin is cold and refreshing. I pluck another apple and another and another until I am bursting with them.

When my belly is full, I shift back, and sleep as a crow on a blanket of grass under the protection of the trees. I do not care who wins the battle beyond the tree line. If the humans find me now, I have already won.

CRETAN QUEST

By DJ Tyrer

A shipful of sacrifices sent
Monster in a maze, Minotaur
Theseus thinks to fight the thing
A gift from Ariadne, aiding the Athenian
Hero and horror head-to-head
Bringing butchery to a brutal end

Sail across the sea as slaves
Menaces men and maidens alike
Through the maze a thread guides Theseus
Allowing access to the antechamber
Hard fought, a horrendous fight hastens
Black sails bring only bad news

EVEN THE DEAD SUFFER

A PRELUDE TO: A VALLEY OF SHADOW

by Lee Patton

Lord Yemor slumped onto a log the villains had conceived to use as a bench. *Peasants. How is it that these sorts never consider stealing decent furniture?* The lord wondered what price he would now pay for anything bearing a cushion. A grimace parted Yemor's lips as he looked at the dead man sitting across from him. He had not even considered what price the corpse would demand. *This undead churl will undoubtedly try to ransom me himself.*

"They were waiting for us." Yemor drank from a half-empty wineskin, then sighed. "Tell me, Izrak Laav. Is there a cure for a wretched soul?"

Seated on a crate, Izrak hunched over his longsword running a whetstone along its edges. The grinding ceased. The dead man peered over the crackling tongues of flame at Yemor. The shadows of his hollowed eyes flickered with the firelight, his lipless grin broad between his desiccated, pallid cheeks.

"Only one that I know of," the dead man said, voice the rasp of wind over an endless sea of sand.

The lord stared at that spectral visage, leaned back and, after a moment, looked away. As if Varon's cells were not torturous enough. This hideous creature was more than Yemor's delicate sensibilities could withstand. *I'm going to flay whoever hired this monster to rescue me.* He waved his hand, laughed.

"That's what I appreciate about you warriors of the Call. Great sense of humor. Always smiling." He chuckled and took another pull of the wine.

Izrak lowered his gaze, resumed sharpening his blade.

Yemor held the wineskin upside-down in front of him, lips pinched, eyes squinting. He shook it. *Empty.* He sighed, tossed the skin to the ground and rose from his seat. The lord stretched his back as he surveyed the carnage on display in the glade. A dozen bodies littered the camp, hewn and maimed. The faces of the brigands were flaxen beneath the full moon, contorted in a fear born not entirely of the wounds they suffered, terrible though they were.

"Did you truly have to do all that?" The lord's arm swept over the scene in a grandiose gesture.

"You did tell those wretched souls to run."

Yemor bent with laughter.

Izrak stowed the whetstone and stood, sliding his sword into its scabbard. "It is time. Those who had the sense to flee will return with more men. We must reach the Myortvi before then." The dull glint on the iron studs of his leather jerkin faded away as he stamped out the fire.

* * *

"Keep low and stay behind me," Izrak said. "The moon's light will be of no help once we are inside."

Yemor trailed him at a cautious distance as they approached the edge of the Myortvi. "Light a torch, then."

The foolish lord did not understand. *The living never can.* The Myortvi—The Dead Woods—was more than some forsaken forest in the borderlands of Enostran. It was a place of evil, of shadow. Ageless and unchanging, the dead wood gave nothing, but only took from those who would travel its tortured paths, piece by piece, until nothing remained. Izrak's journeys carried him through the dark wood with relative frequency, and the mercenary would often wonder, as he trudged beneath its abyssal canopy, if he should not simply remain. In the end, what more could the dead wood take? Was that place not fitting for one such as him? Countless arcane horrors prowled that realm of perpetual dusk, and none suffered the light to pass within its fetid reaches. *Why did she send us this way?* Any sign of life would be consumed.

"No fire."

"Then how are we supposed to see, Izrak? We'll be lost for sure." Yemor stopped, placed his pudgy hands on his hips. "Well?"

Izrak continued a few paces, then halted. Standing deathly still, he faced away from the lord as his fingers closed around a frayed pouch on his belt. *Lost ... For over three centuries, you have held me in your grasp. Why will you not show me the way? Why do you keep me blind?* After a moment, he shifted his dead gaze upon the quivering lord. The mercenary's eyes were black pits, features ephemeral in the silver light of the moon.

"The darkness holds no secrets from me."

Lord Yemor quickened his pace, shuffling behind the mercenary as he moved on. "Easy for you … What does a corpse have to fear?"

"I fear many things."

Yemor snorted. "But how could you be afraid? You're already dead."

Izrak stopped before a mangled tree at the wood's edge, warped, twisted beyond recognition, its blackened bark peeling away in curling strips. *Just like me.* He ran his pale, skeletal fingers over the shriveled bark. "Even the dead can suffer." A flutter of wings drew his attention skyward; a murder of crows, concealed within night's black shroud, flitted by overhead from the direction of the brigand's campsite, their midnight meal disturbed by unwelcome intruders. *Perhaps I have lingered here for too long …* A hollow sigh passed from the mercenary as he drew his sword, its nicked, razor edges gleaming in the moonlight. "Come, my lord. Varon's men will not be far behind."

"Must we go through these wretched woods? Surely there must be another way." Yemor retreated a step, staring at the gnarled, barren branches reaching into the night—fingers of the damned clawing out of some ancient hell.

The mercenary glanced left, then right. "There are. Three of them." Izrak adjusted his worn-leather skullcap. "We can go around, two leagues to the north, three to the south. Or we could make it easy for Varon, and simply go back."

Trembling beneath his thick, sable furs, Lord Yemor peered back down the serpentine path. He breathed in deep, released it. "The woods, then."

"So be it. Hold onto my belt. Do not let go."

Yemor reached a shaking, hesitant hand toward the mercenary.

Izrak grunted. "Fear not. There are worse terrors in these woods than I."

A screeching howl pierced the dread silence of the night. Answering calls echoed throughout the dark wood.

"What was that?" Yemor said, grasping the mercenary's belt.

Izrak looked over his shoulder, his maw drawn in its eternal grin of rotted, yellow teeth. "Guuls."

* * *

The darkness was suffocating. Although, it may simply have been the rancid stench of the corpse shambling ahead as the lord trailed behind. All around, branches rattled in the fell wind, twigs snapped, and owls sang in unseen congregation—a solemn dirge for the passing of two lost souls. Yemor pinched the bridge of his nose, finger and thumb coming away slick with sweat. *How can he see in this?* A dull pain throbbed at the backs of his eyes, the strain of peering into the preternatural black of the woods plaguing the lord with a headache. *How much longer must I suffer this place? This corpse?*

"Are we almost out?"

"Quiet," the dead man said. His frame went rigid beneath his jerkin and mail coat. He stopped.

The lord stumbled into him, like walking into a stone wall. Yemor grunted. "What is it?"

Izrak gave no reply.

Useless though it was, Yemor flicked his gaze from side to side. He scowled, furrowed his brow. The owls' song had fallen away. The winds ceased, the woods, still. His skin broke out with gooseflesh. Suddenly, a scratching—claws dragging over wood—tore through the silence. Shivering, the lord snapped his head in the direction of the horrid sound. A branch cracked. Yemor yelped, slapped a hand over his mouth.

A keening wail shattered the turgid air. Rapid footfalls charged in from the right, the attendant wail growing louder. Yemor flinched as the noise drew closer. The air whistled on the edge of a blade—the wail cut off in an instant. Foul blood spattered over the lord's cheek. His nails bit into bloodless palms as his grip tightened on the dead man's belt.

The Myortvi erupted in a storm of ripping claws and ravenous cries. "Run." Izrak took off.

Stumbling after the mercenary, clinging desperately to his belt, Yemor's stout legs struggled in a terrified frenzy to keep pace. Horror closed in on all sides as clicking fangs and blood-curdling shrieks haunted each step. But every time the monsters came near, they were consumed by the whip and whistle of Izrak's sword as it sang its song of death.

And yet, the number of the wretched guuls seemed to increase. Sweat, now mixed with blood, poured over Yemor's brow, his ragged breaths coming in wheezing gasps. The dead man stopped, and the lord crashed into him. Yemor's stiff fingers slipped from Izrak's belt as he was sent sprawling across the ground.

"Damn you, hell-spawn." Heart hammering in his chest, he threw out his hands in a flailing attempt to retake hold of his macabre guardian. Yemor's fingers found cold flesh. "Izrak?"

Claws gripped the lord's shoulders, pinning him to the ground as a hot breath washed over his face in rank waves. Yemor shriveled and whimpered, a feral snarl the only reply. The creature's obscured face hung over his own. Yemor's fingers sank into the cold mud as jagged fangs brushed against his neck.

"Izrak …" he said, throat choked with fear and disgust. *That monster abandoned me, left me to die.* "Help me!"

A whistling slice fell from above, ending in a dull smack of steel on flesh. The snarling ended in a whine. Hot blood sprayed the lord's face as the monster's body slumped against his, then rolled away.

A hand closed around the collar of Yemor's tunic, pulling the lord to his feet in one fluid motion. "On your … feet," the dead man rasped.

Yemor ran a hand over his face, wiping away the blood, his body quaking as his mouth opened and closed wordlessly.

"Need to … run …"

"Just get me out of here!" The lord felt Izrak's hand tighten on his collar before pulling him closer. The dead man's hand trembled. Yemor's skin crawled. He heard the grinding clatter of teeth just above his head. His stomach twisted as the lord tried to back away, but the dead man held him fast. "Unhand me, corpse." Frigid fingers closed around his throat.

Branches split as a mass of screeching fury collided with the dead man. Yemor heard the hollow thud of Izrak's sword hitting the mud as his hand was torn away from the lord's throat. "Izrak!" Yemor staggered back, hearing claws rake over chainmail amid the guuls' wails and snapping jaws. He turned, about to run, when a very human roar exploded from the shadows. The lord froze as terror turned his blood to ice.

The bloody squelch of tearing flesh and the ripping crack of breaking bones assailed the lord's senses. *Just get me out of here …* The howling of the guuls turned to fearful whines before being stifled one by one. *Don't let them take me …* Yemor closed his eyes, hearing teeth sinking into meat as he covered his ears. *Not like this …*

After a time, Yemor opened his eyes, and held his hands out in front of him. All was quiet in the dead wood once more. The lord stumbled forward a step. "Izrak? Are you there? What the hell happened to you?"

A pair of yellow orbs, dim embers smoldering in the shadows, materialized several paces away. Mud squelched beneath heavy boots as the orbs rose slowly to the height of a tall man. The embers burned out. Disembodied steps approached the lord. Yemor heard the rattle of mail, then the clack of a sword falling into its scabbard. A fell presence lingered in front of him, its dead chill prickling his flesh.

"Come, my lord. We are near the end." Izrak's rasp seethed from the black.

"What about the guuls?" Yemor said. "Surely there are more of them. We won't make it."

"They will trouble us no longer."

"How do you know?"

"They are afraid."

* * *

Flickering torchlight and the nervous chatter of Lord Yemor's retinue greeted them as Izrak led the nobleman out of the Myortvi. A carriage sat on the rough trail, surrounded by two-dozen mounted men-at-arms. As the mercenary and his charge approached, a figure emerged from the carriage, hooded and cloaked in black. *Always with me.* The mercenary's pace slowed, fingers closing around his age-worn pouch.

"So, it was you who hired this corpse to rescue me." Yemor strode forward as Izrak stopped a few paces away. "Lady Olesia."

At this, the lady lowered her hood. Olesia's raven hair shimmered in the firelight, bound at the crown with a silver circlet, a rich amethyst at its center glittering upon her porcelain brow. Her ashen eyes were storms, roiling clouds streaked with flecks of violet lightning. The corners of her mauve lips curled upward as she closed her eyes and bowed.

Lord Yemor chuckled. "And what was the promised payment?"

Lady Olesia leaned in, whispered in his ear.

The lord snorted. "Is that all?" Yemor laughed as he moved past Olesia towards the carriage. "Very well." He climbed inside. "And to think, I would've given him a castle, but I suppose a tomb is more fitting for a corpse." The lord sneered, slamming the carriage door shut.

Izrak held Olesia's gaze as she stepped closer to him. The lady stared into the empty pits of his eyes, a smile creeping into her lips. *What does she see there?* A moment passed. The lady drew a tattered, browned scroll from the folds of her sleeve, and held it out to him.

Izrak took the scroll. "The location. It is inside?"

The lady nodded, then held out a small leather purse. Izrak tilted his head. Olesia stepped forward, took his hand and placed the purse on his palm. The mercenary stared into Olesia's eyes as his fingers closed around it. "Thank you." Her hand held his for a heartbeat, for two. She let go.

Olesia pulled her hood over her head and turned away. She climbed into the carriage, and the lord's retinue departed. Several of the men-at-arms cast glances back at the mercenary as they rode along the trail.

Izrak watched for a time as the cavalcade faded into the gloom on the horizon. *Olesia* … The moon hung low over the foothills rolling in the west, its pale light giving way to the crimson of encroaching dawn. *In another time, perhaps* … His fingers played along the woven surface of the pouch at his hip, the Record of Kosh clutched in the other hand. *At last, I will find you.* The mercenary placed the scroll in his satchel. He turned and trudged along the Myortvi towards the jagged peaks rising in the north, the Crown of Yaros. *And my suffering will finally come to an end.*

* * *

Following chapters of *A Valley of Shadow* will be published to our website (magazine.thearcanist.net) on the last Friday of the month, starting February 28, 2025, and running to its conclusion on June 27, 2025.

A Valley of Shadow Publication Schedule

Part One: 28 Feb., 2025

Part Two: 28 March, 2025

Part Three: 24 April, 2025

Part Four: 30 May, 2025

Part Five: 27 June, 2025

Paperback and Hardcover Release: 31 Oct., 2025

Contributors

Alicia Alves (she/her) is a Canadian speculative fiction writer. She has written fiction for most of her life, and she has a Ph.D. in English. Her work has been published in *The Wise Owl* and is forthcoming in the *Dead Girls Walking* anthology by *Wicked Shadow Press*.

Aubrey Zahn is an artist, activist, and attorney who decided to try her hand at writing something other than legal memoranda. Her fantasy and science fiction stories have been published in *Queer Science Fiction, Myths Subverted,* and the anthology *Dark Cheer: Cryptids Emerging*.

Courtney Chester is currently a second-year Professional Writing graduate student at Kennesaw State University (KSU). She is one of the founding members for KSU's Narrative Game Lab and their first game, *Corporation Inc.*, was recently released. Her work has been published in *The Greyhound Journal*.

DJ Tyrer is the person behind Atlantean Publishing, editor of *View From Atlantis*, and has been published in *Gargoylicon, Lycanthropicon,* and *Vampiricon*, and issues of *Enchanted Conversation, The Horrorzine, Journ-E, Lovecraftiana, Scifaikuest, Sirens Call, Star*Line,* and *Tigershark*.

Website: djtyrer.blogspot.co.uk

Facebook: facebook.com/DJTyrerwriter/

Frank William Finney is a poet from Massachusetts who taught literature in Thailand for 25 years. A joint winner of The Letter Review Prize for Poetry, his poems have appeared in *Blue Unicorn, Hare's Paw Literary Journal, Persephone Literary Magazine, Tales of the Strange*, and elsewhere. His chapbook *The Folding of the Wings* was published in 2022 (FLP Books).

Twitter (X): @finneyfw

Instagram: @fwfinney

Grant Sable hails from a region of rainfall. A stalwart lover of blood and mansions, he enjoys exploring the beauty of the macabre.

James Callan is the author of the novel *A Transcendental Habit* (Queer Space, 2023). His fiction has appeared in *Barzakh Magazine, BULL, Carte Blanche, Hawaii Pacific Review, Mystery Tribune,* and elsewhere. He lives on the Kāpiti Coast, Aotearoa New Zealand.

James D. Mills resides in Bloomington, Indiana. He lives a slow life of self-sufficiency with his partner, Eden, and their growing family. After losing his mother to brain cancer, he writes fantasy and contemporary literature that tackles the complexities of loss, healing, and community. Soon he will earn his bachelor's in Creative Writing and Psychology from Southern New Hampshire University. His work has been published by *The Penmen Review, Floyd County Moonshine, Calliope,* among others.

Website: jamesdmills.com

John Mueter is a pianist, composer, educator and writer residing in Kansas City, Missouri. His short fiction has appeared in many journals, most recently in *The First Line, The Corona Book of Ghost Storie,s* and *The Mason Street Journal,* poetry in *The Train River Anthology* and *The Bombay Literary Magazine.* A collection of stories and poems, "Last Days" has recently been published and is available at Amazon.com.

Website: johnmueter.wordpress.com

Lee Patton is a Christian and United States Army veteran pursuing an education in creative writing and English. He is at home in the realm of fantasy, where anything is possible. When not sending his heroes on legendary adventures, he is reading, improving his craft, and learning the Russian language.

Maria Spence has been an educator in four countries, mainly teaching high school and middle school English. Heading into the second half of her life, she hopes to spend less time teaching others to write and more time doing it herself.

Menke HB was born in The Netherlands, yet English became her heart language before she moved to the USA in her early 20s. When she is not busy homeschooling her four kids, Menke enjoys reading and writing long and short-form speculative fiction, creative nonfiction, and poetry.

T. J. Young is a writer living in Seattle, WA. He occasionally travels to the Andromeda galaxy in search of material, but otherwise spends most of his time reading. He is married with three superhero children.

William L. Ramsey (he/him) is a Professor at Lander University. His poems have appeared in *Beloit Poetry Journal, Hampden-Sydney Poetry Review, Poetry East, Poetry Magazine, Poetry Northwest, The South Carolina Review*, and *Southern Poetry Review*. His first book of poetry, *Dilemmas*, is available from Clemson University Press.

Rise Above Stories

Lessons in Tragedy and Triumph
as Told by Those Who Inspire Change

Rise Above Stories is a platform intended to spread awareness by sharing personal stories with an emphasis on fostering **connection, empathy, and understanding** among individuals.

Being a narrator can be a profound experience, bringing validation and connection, awareness and education, advocacy and change, inspiration and hope, and ultimately, healing and empowerment.

Share your story with us.

Reach us on Facebook at Rise Above Stories
Text us at (812) 361-0443 or email us at Riseabovestories@icloud.com

This page was left intentionally blank
Feel free to write notes here.

PANDEMONIUM AWAITS.

ASHEN RIDER by James D. Mills releases in Paperback on December 19th, 2025.

This novel will run as a serial on our website beginning July 31, 2025.

James D. Mills

What Lies Below

A Dusk and Dawn Novel

HOW DO YOU REBULD AFTER YOU LIFE FALLS APART?.

WHAT LIES BELOW by James D. Mills releases in Paperback on
November 11th, 2025.

A Valley of Shadow

A VALLEY OF SHADOW by Lee Patton is a modern take on classic Sword and Sorcery that releases on October 31, 2025.

Read the entire novel free: magazine.thearcanist.net/a-valley-of-shadow-part-one

For the undead warriors of The Call, existence itself is a crime, their service to the sinister lords of Enostran, a punishment. Those who disobey are swiftly destroyed, and the warriors of The Call tend to their own. Izrak Laav, a veteran mercenary of many long centuries, is tasked with the destruction of one such rogue warrior